Qwan

THE SHOWDOWN

written by

juvenile

Los Angeles

CONTEMPORARY BOOKS

Chicago

Dedicated to Walia and Niko

Cover illustration by Richard Kirk
Cover photograph © C. Rosenstein/Photonica

Library of Congress Catalog Card Number is available.
ISBN: 1-56565-558-3

Publisher: Jack Artenstein
Associate Publisher, Juvenile Division: Elizabeth D. Amos
Director of Publishing Services: Rena Copperman
Managing Editor: Lindsey Hay
Art Director: Lisa-Theresa Lenthall
Cover and Interior Design: Cheryl Carrington

Roxbury Park is an imprint of Lowell House,
A Division of the RGA Publishing Group, Inc.

Lowell House books can be purchased at special discounts
when ordered in bulk for premiums and special sales.
Contact Department JH at the following address:

Lowell House Juvenile
2029 Century Park East
Suite 3290
Los Angeles, CA 90067

Manufactured in the United States of America
10 9 8 7 6 5 4 3 2 1

A brother offended is harder to be won than a strong city: and their contentions are like the bars of a castle.

Proverbs 18:19

prologue

First there were two great nations, one in the East, the other in the West, at odds over a third, smaller nation. Despite their combined efforts, the superpowers failed to agree on a workable solution to the conflict, and after a short period of time, the threat of war became a chilling reality. Soon panic and fear seized both countries, and each began taking precautionary steps should the unthinkable come to pass.

On the West Coast of the United States, government officials designated several areas as safe zones. One such region was the great desert basin, where thousands of parents brought their children to wait out the threat of war while they returned to their homes and their duty.

The desert children sat in the dark as their food supply began to run low, and news of the war slowed to a trickle. Then there was no longer any communication with the outside at all.

On a windy, sand-swept night, the desert sky let down a horrible curtain of blinding white light. Strange illnesses followed in the wake of the blast, and the few adults in the desert were the first taken by the dreadful sickness.

Those children who were left scrambled to survive by whatever means possible, watching and waiting as the world around them grew quiet.

Part One
INTO THE WOODS

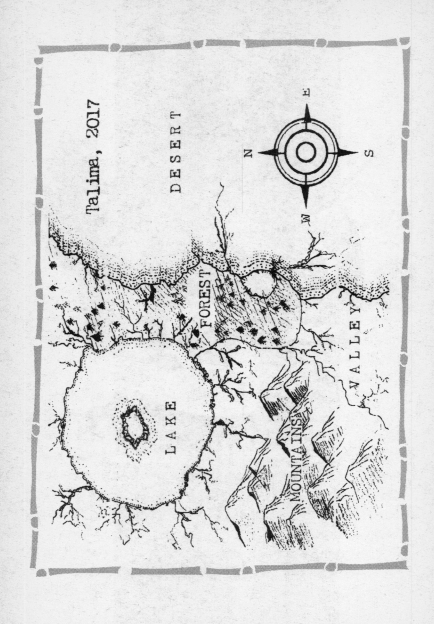

chapter 1

The Pacific Northwest, 2017

He had been waiting outside since darkness had settled over Talima, standing in the alley next to the Red Rain Tavern with its lifeless neon sign over the doorway.

Waiting for his luck to change.

Thirteen-year-old Qwan Lee poked his head out from the shadows and glanced up and down the desolate pavement of Main Street. The man he was waiting for was nowhere in sight, and Qwan was beginning to grow impatient, nervous. His calf muscles ached, blisters on both feet burned, and for the first time doubts began to creep into his mind like a shadowy intruder.

It was midsummer, and the heat from earlier in the day had scarcely abated, hovering now just above ninety-five degrees. The heat caught in Qwan's throat and choked him like a noose. His tattered black T-shirt was thoroughly soaked, and a mixture of sweat and dirt streamed down the sides of his face and collected in the corners of his mouth.

Main Street remained silent, still. A light mist rose stealthily from the scorched asphalt.

Talima wasn't much of a town, he thought, stepping back into the shadows, flattening his back against the warm wall of the Red Rain Tavern. Main Street—the town's only street—stretched only about a hundred yards along the fringe of a dense green-black forest and was lined on either side by squat log houses, buildings that were made to resemble dwellings from the nineteenth century. The street was cloaked in darkness; the narrow alleys and storefronts were tumbledown, chaotic; and weeds grew in every crack and crevice.

Qwan concentrated on the alley directly across the street, on the narrow dirt path between the now-deserted Talima Indian Museum and a vacant souvenir shop. The path trailed some fifty feet west until it was swallowed up by the forest. That's where he had last seen the man, the man he was waiting for.

He peeked around the corner. The harsh glow of the moon reflected insanely over his face, illuminating the long black bangs that hung over his eyes like jungle vines. He shook out his hands, rotated the muscles in his neck and shoulders, and waited.

Reaching into the waistband of his pants, Qwan took out a small bottle, unscrewed the top and poured a few drops of warm water into his mouth—just enough to ward off his thirst. The liquid spread over his tongue, mouth, and down his throat. He savored the sensation, tilting his head upward and drinking in the starlight with his eyes.

He was used to the heat; four miserable years roaming the desert had prepared him for worse. Even so he had noticed the summer months were getting hotter and the winters bitterly cold.

The extreme weather was just one harsh reality of this new world. Hunger was another.

As Qwan stood alone in the pitch-black alley, hunger gripped every cell in his taut body. He knew hunger as one knows a brother or sister, knew its tendencies, its levels. For five years it had been his shadow, a merciless presence that followed him everywhere. But like most survivors, Qwan had come to accept the empty feeling in his gut as inevitable—even when it gnawed at his insides like a wild dog and caused him to double over in pain. There was very little he could do about it.

His mind was murky, unfocused. It was as if two conflicting realities, past and present, were fighting over his thoughts, battling for his attention and making him anxious, making him not want to think at all.

He had felt this way ever since he entered Talima earlier that evening. Actually, it was Billy who had first spotted the town. Billy Tex was Qwan's friend. The two had arrived in Talima just before sunset. They had been walking west from the desert for close to a week, through shifting sand dunes and tumbling sagebrush. They'd explored abandoned horse corrals and deserted shacks, salvaging whatever they could and living only on the meat of jackrabbits and tasteless white flowers. After years of roaming the desolate wasteland they had crawled out of their desert graves because they had to believe there was something more to the world than the hopelessness they had known since the end of the war. Their plan was to head west, out of the desert to the forests before starting the long trek south to their homes—or what was left of them.

On the fifth day of their travels, when the landscape had begun to turn a lush green, when the trees grew larger and leafier, they had picked up a highway. They followed it for several hours until Billy Tex wearily raised an arm and pointed down a narrow side road. As they climbed the steeply paved road and reached the wooden gate bearing the name "Talima" chiseled in one of the logs, frigid shreds of memories began filtering through Qwan's mind like a puff of cold air beneath a doorway. He looked up and saw the forest behind the street, its forbidding green front standing guard like an army of giant soldiers. Then he remembered.

There was still no sign of the man. Qwan turned to

face the wall of the Red Rain Tavern. He would leave
soon, he thought, wiping sweat from his forehead. He
would leave because Billy would be wondering where
he was, and because Talima was making him remember
too much.

Memory, he often thought, was an undesirable
thing. It was a destructive force that only paralyzed the
mind with fear and misery. Memories were demons—
tempting and fleeting and slippery as a lie. They had to
be controlled if you had any hope of surviving in this
new world. For Qwan, these demons were so potent,
so threatening, that it was as if he kept them sealed in
a box somewhere deep in the recesses of his brain, shut
off from the present where they could only bring him
harm. He had been able to control them in the desert,
where survival had occupied his every thought. But that
had changed the moment he had arrived in Talima. As
he poked his head out from the shadows of the dark
alley, as his eyes strained in the blind darkness, for the
first time in a long time he felt his control beginning to
slip, and the seal on the box coming unglued.

He had been to Talima before. Once before.

He had been to the national park in the middle of
nowhere, the scenic tourist attraction where once
hundreds of families came every day to enjoy the peace
and tranquility of its natural surroundings. Here the
forest and lake and adjoining canyon had been spared
the decay of surrounding civilization. Pristine Talima,

where things had remained the same as when the Indians had roamed the land, and where Qwan's parents had taken him and his older brother on a weekend camping trip several months before the world changed forever.

But that was before the war, before families were separated and lives were changed forever.

It wasn't that the memories from that weekend were particularly significant. They weren't. In fact, he remembered very little about the camping trip. But these memories bred other, more significant ones, memories of his family and of his home, things he had long ago resolved to forget.

He heard a noise coming from behind him in the alley. A rattling sound, like metal or tin. Hands raised, knees slightly bent, he whirled around and immediately spotted its source. A bony rat had scurried out from a rusted old can that lay in the weeds at the base of the Red Rain Tavern. His heart racing, Qwan watched the rodent's tail probing the air as the creature wriggled out the back of the alley in fits and starts. He took a few deep breaths and shook out his hands.

Fear.

He had learned how to deal with fear. He wouldn't have made it this far without accomplishing that much. You don't lose everything you ever had and live in poverty and despair and chaos without conquering fear and doubt. He had done this, and it had allowed him to survive. He was standing in a pitch-black alley of a ghost town because he had learned to quell his fears, to suppress his feelings, to forget about the past, about the war and about his family.

And about his older brother—the last family member he had seen alive.

Clouds raced over the moon and for a moment there was absolutely no light over Main Street. Darkness didn't bother Qwan. The shapes, the outlines, the movement of all these things, the blending and shifting of the natural tide of night—these were the things you had to know in order to live in a world without electricity. So he stared out into the black and waited for his sixth sense to kick in. Waited for light to come from darkness.

He felt his entire body beginning to stiffen. Keeping his eyes glued to the street, he stretched down and grabbed behind each ankle, folding his torso straight down over his legs. He held that position for several seconds when his thoughts suddenly turned to Billy.

His friend would be worried.

The trip out of the desert had taken a toll on Billy. And when they had arrived in Talima, Billy had settled down beneath the canopy of a huge fir tree by the front gate. Qwan had chosen to explore the small town while there was still light. He had dropped his bundle beside his friend's and stepped cautiously through the gate, assuring Billy that he would return before long.

Several moments after he'd left Billy, Qwan had climbed down the west side of the ridge and emerged onto the street. It was then that he'd spotted the man about a hundred yards ahead, walking in the same direction, an empty grey sack slung over his shoulder.

Qwan had taken cover against the broad side of the boarded-up Talima Post Office. He knew he was grasping at straws, but he had a feeling the man would lead him to something—anything. Maybe even food. So he'd decided to follow close behind and see what happened.

He was swift and light and he'd managed to draw within twenty yards without being noticed when the man had taken a left turn between the souvenir shop and the Indian museum. On the other side of the street stood the Red Rain Tavern. In the enfolding darkness Qwan had stepped into the alley next to the tavern and pressed his back up against the wall, watching as the man had walked down the path toward the forest and vanished.

And so here he was, hiding in the dark some thirty minutes later, waiting for some phantom who might never show because what people did in Talima was a mystery to him. And if he had learned one thing in this new and dangerous world, it was that caution was the only policy.

He took out a pocket watch from his pants pocket and smirked.

The absurdity of time. His brother had given him the watch as a gift on his seventh birthday. That was six years ago. On the face of the watch in black and white was the Chinese yin-yang symbol, symbolizing two opposing forces of life that nevertheless could not exist without each other. The crystal was cracked and scratched from numerous falls and scrapes but the time, as far as Qwan knew, had remained accurate. The world had been turned upside down but the watch was in perfect condition.

In the darkened alley Qwan raised the watch to his ear and listened to the faint ticking and decided that he hated the watch, hated everything about it. He would throw it away, or bury it, because he hated it so much. The ticking drummed in his ear and filled his brain with a consuming hate, and it was only by chance that he turned in time to see a figure emerging from the dark alley across the street.

He shoved the watch back in his pocket, shoved it all the way down, making sure it was deep and snug and safe.

His pulse began to race as he watched the man emerge from the woods behind the log houses, coming into the alley between the Indian museum and the souvenir shop.

Steeling himself, Qwan focused on the large grey sack slung over the man's shoulder, now bulging. He had been right about the man. He had been right to wait. His legs trembled just perceptibly as he shook out his arms.

The man, an African American, wore a torn brown tank top, army pants, and a pair of ratty old black boots with rags for laces. As he stepped into the street by the museum, he suddenly reached down and grabbed hold of one knee.

Qwan looked on with curiosity, standing in the shadows, waiting for his luck to change.

chapter 2

Peter Humphrey grabbed his knee and waited for the pain to subside. He shouldn't have run so fast, but the incident in the woods had taken him by surprise. Now the twenty-year-old African American stood on the corner of Main Street next to the Indian museum, catching his breath.

And happy to be out of the woods.

He had been stripping berries from a bush about a quarter mile into the forest when he heard the sound. It was a hissing sound, the sound of something unseen sweeping through the scrub behind him. When he turned he saw nothing. He was thankful for that. But it was dark and he had no light, so he couldn't be too sure of anything. He had started late from the valley and had found himself living his worst nightmare: being in the forest in the dark—alone.

Fortunately the sack was nearly filled. And even though Peter realized the fear was probably all in his head, he had wasted no time leaving the scene. He had stuffed another cluster of red berries into the sack, twirled the end shut, and started down the trail toward Main Street.

As a Tribe member Peter was happy to contribute to the cause, whether by fetching wood and sticks for burning or helping to set up for the monthly tournament. It felt good to help out, he often thought, but fetching berries was another matter. Fetching berries meant going into the woods, where Llao lived.

Peter had been a member of the Tribe for almost two years, and he'd heard many stories about the giant beast that roamed the forest. One such story said that Llao was a product of the war, a kind of mutant bear or wolf. Others insisted that he was a man—that is, he had once been a man. Peter didn't believe in any one story more than another. But he hated the woods nonetheless. He had grown up in the city, in Los Angeles, and in the woods he was lost.

Very few men could intimidate Peter Humphrey. He was an imposing figure, standing close to six feet tall and skilled in the martial arts. But the forest was another story. And as he ran down the dark trail, branches lashing his arms and face, he'd felt a sudden twinge in his knee—a jolt of pain caused by an old martial arts injury.

Now, hunched over, he waited for the pain to subside, glancing back at the forest behind him.

Qwan

Over the years Peter had been through many battles, and his body had begun to feel their ill effects. Opponents had broken his nose three times, fractured all his fingers and toes, cracked his ribs, punctured his eardrums, and broken his kneecap.

But his vision remained as sharp as ever.

By the time he straightened up and resumed his walk down Main Street, he had already spotted the Asian boy hiding in the shadows across the street and had begun considering various self-defense techniques should the occasion to use them present itself.

It did.

The boy jumped out from the alley and stood before him with raised fists. "Give me the bag," he demanded, staring into Peter's eyes with a look of contempt.

Peter didn't move. He stood in the middle of the dark street with his legs far apart, rubbing his chin as though struggling with some infinitely complicated math problem. "You don't know what you're doing, little man," he said, grinning. "Nobody steals from the Tribe, and nobody steals from Jack Mann." He cracked his knuckles and raised his fists.

For a moment the boy stopped in his tracks. A puzzled expression stole over his face. It was as if something Peter said had awaken in him some long-lost memory.

Peter didn't know what to make of the boy. He lowered his guard and placed his hands on his hips. "What's your discipline, little guy? Karate? Kung-fu? Jujutsu?"

"Just throw me the sack."

The boy's insolence surprised Peter, who rubbed his large hands together and began to loosen the muscles in his neck. A trace of a smile appeared on his face, as if he were savoring something pleasant. "Come get it."

Qwan stepped to within a few feet of Peter, who for the first time got a good look at the boy's eyes. They were black. Black with hatred. And they locked onto Peter's eyes and never let go.

"Listen," Peter warned. "You're in way over your head. We don't tolerate thieves in Talima. I'll tell you what . . . take off now, and I'll forget this ever happened. Otherwise—"

In one swift motion Qwan skipped forward and thrust out a side kick at Peter's disabled knee. Caught off guard, Peter lowered an arm to block the kick—a kick that never arrived.

Stupid, Peter thought, too late. His head and torso were bent slightly forward, fully exposed. The fake kick to his knee had pulled him out of position. It was an amateur's mistake, and one that would cost Peter dearly.

What happened next was a blur. Suddenly the boy was airborne, his feet nearly level with Peter's chest—his entire body spinning with the velocity of a tornado before exploding with a kick that caught Peter flush on his cheek. The blow dropped the larger man to the steamy asphalt.

Peter Humphrey had been fighting practically since the day he was born. He'd seen and fought against some very tough martial artists. But he'd never seen anything like this. No one this quick.

His vision blurred. Peter lifted his aching head just in time to stop a few berries rolling toward him on the pavement. A few feet away, the boy was gathering up the spilled berries and shoving them back into the sack.

Peter tried to lift himself off the ground. "You're not just stealing from the Tribe," he said groggily. "You're stealing from Jack Mann." Then he fell back down, watching as the boy disappeared into the gloom of Main Street.

Peter felt the swelling coming under his left eye. So many thoughts stirred in his brain. As far as he knew, no member of the Tribe had ever been robbed before. This would be the first time, and it had been on his watch.

He knelt down on the ground, his head throbbing. Despite how serious tonight's events might be, Peter could only think of the boy, could only think of the speed and intensity and cunning of the boy. He had witnessed something truly awesome.

And he suspected he would see it again.

chapter 3

T_hud!_

Billy sat bolt upright and strained his eyes in the darkness. "Huh!" he muttered, half asleep.

Qwan had dropped the sack on the ground beside Billy. He knelt down and opened a hand revealing the dark-red berries. "Not very much, but it will do for now," he said.

"What took you so long?" Billy asked, rubbing his eyes. He reached around Qwan's hand and grabbed a handful of berries from the sack.

"I had to wait. That's all."

Billy stopped chewing, pushed back his shoulder-length dirty-blond hair and stared at his friend long and hard. He knew Qwan, knew when he was holding something back. His eyes grew wide. "You got into a fight, didn't you?"

Qwan looked up at the crest of the forest to the south, dark against the moonlit sky. He knew what was coming; he had been through it many times. Still there was something about its reliability that appealed to him.

"Come on," Billy whined. "You should've come to get me. Someday you're gonna need my help, man. Then what are you gonna do?" He jumped to his feet and turned to face Qwan. "Check this out." Billy bent his knees and began throwing punches at the air straight ahead, one after another, counting in muffled grunts until he reached ten. "There," he said, catching his breath. "What do ya think?"

"I think you should sit down."

Dejected, Billy settled back down near his bundle on the ground. Sitting with his knees drawn into his chest, he looked out over the front gate of Talima and beyond. His face suddenly took on a grave expression. "What do you think it's like out there now? Ya know, in the rest of the country?"

Qwan looked away. This question was also something he was used to hearing from Billy. Not that it bothered Qwan. It was just that he thought it strange that Billy should be so concerned with such things, things that were beyond their control. There was nothing they could do about it—nothing anybody could do about it—and in the ever-present context of survival, it was hardly even relevant.

Qwan preferred not to talk about such things. But since he felt kind of like Billy's older brother, even though they were both thirteen, he tried his best to answer his friend's questions, to make him feel better when he seemed to be down.

Now Qwan tried to think of an answer to an impossible question: Was anything left? It was an answer he could not possibly know. Besides, something else was on his mind, something he couldn't put his finger on, but it was there, buzzing around his brain like a fly. It was something the man in the street had said. Someone's name—a name that was somehow familiar to him.

"Well, what do you think?" Billy pressed. "Do ya think our parents are still alive out there?"

Qwan grabbed his things and stood up. "I think we should get moving."

Billy sighed. "You've got to talk more, man," he said, exasperated. "Why don't ya ever talk about the past, Qwan? About your family . . . or your brother?"

"Shut up, Billy," Qwan snapped, not meaning to be so harsh. He quickly reached down and placed a hand on Billy's shoulder. "Look, I just don't see how those things are important any more. That's all." He paused for a moment. "Listen, we really do have to move."

"Why?" Billy insisted.

"The guy I took these berries from might not be alone," Qwan replied. "He said something about belonging to a tribe. Probably just made it up, but we shouldn't take any chances. Anyway, we're too out in the open here. Let's cross the road and go down near the woods, find a safe place to sleep for the night."

Billy looked at Qwan for a long minute, shrugged, then rolled up his blanket.

They started down the grassy ridge toward the forest, holding their bundles under their arms. Passing the front gate of Talima, they continued west, walking about a hundred yards till they cleared a low hill. The forest rose before them. Billy clung to the sack of berries. Qwan kept an eye on Main Street.

As they approached the woods, they heard an owl hooting and the sound of water trickling over rocks. A narrow creek came into view, nestled between the fringe of the forest and the base of the hill. It was clear and shallow and ran out from the forest, trailing along its edge to the south. Qwan remembered the creek. He also remembered that if he followed it south, the creek would cut back into the woods and come out in a valley on the other side. He remembered taking a hike with his father and brother through the woods and the valley.

When they reached the creek, Qwan threw off his bundle and got down on all fours. *Plenty of water around here*, he thought, *plenty of water and plenty of food*. He kneeled over the brook and submerged his face in the cool water. Small grey and brown rocks covered the floor of the creek, and flimsy green plants swayed in the lazy current. Qwan drank for nearly thirty seconds, filling his stomach, all the while thinking about the incident on the street. Something was bothering him.

Then it came to him. He pulled his head out of the water and wiped his eyes. Jack Mann. That was the name the stranger had spoken. Qwan was sure he had heard the name before, but he couldn't place it. He looked at Billy, who was kneeling over the creek a few feet away, cupping handfuls of water and gulping them down.

Jack Mann.

Qwan hadn't told Billy he had been to Talima before. There hadn't been a reason to tell him. He had figured they would only stay the night and start the long trip south in the morning. But now he wasn't quite sure. There was something about Talima, something hidden in the brooding forest and the stark street, some secret that he couldn't quite grasp, but it was there, sure as he was alive.

In the desert Qwan had promised Billy they would try to return to their homes in the city in the south, where both boys had lived before the war. And Qwan intended to fulfill his promise.

In time.

He lay back against the earth and reached over for the sack of berries. The sky over the forest was like a vast field of signs, all blinking and alive. He breathed in the warm air, drawing it deep into his lungs—a satisfied breath.

Qwan dropped a berry in his mouth and locked his arms around the back of his head.

His luck, for the moment, had changed.

chapter 4

Orange flames fluttered on top of five-foot torches posted around the dirt clearing on the valley floor. Shadows from the flames quivered and quaked, rising up over the dozens of small tents and shacks that dotted the far side of the valley, and dancing like dark phantoms on the wall of trees above. The air was muggy and still.

Inside the dirt clearing, Jhoon, the eighteen-year-old Asian American leader of the Tribe, settled into a side stance as his three attackers crept closer. He eyed the biggest of the three cautiously.

The man, whose beard and mustache were a bright orange, stood over six feet, with thick forearms and knuckles the size of walnuts. Sweat poured into his mustache and down the sides of his fleshy cheeks. The early evening heat was suffocating, and the big man constantly wiped sweat from his eyes.

Jhoon would take him out first.

The second one to worry about was a brown-skinned girl with straight brown hair down to the middle of her back. Her movements were fluid, graceful. Arms extended, her fingers tapped the air as if she were playing an imaginary flute. As she inched toward Jhoon on one side, she shifted the balance of her weight so perfectly that she appeared to be floating above the ground.

On Jhoon's other side, a lanky boy with a shaved head and hollow cheeks approached. Unlike the girl, he stood erect, his movements rigid. His green eyes were heavy-lidded, and a jagged purplish vein ran down the middle of his forehead, pulsating with each breath he took. His name was Bud, and he held his hands in front of his face, fists clenched, like a boxer.

Jhoon Lee followed all of their movements carefully, tracking them with calm, steady eyes—unrevealing eyes.

There were others present—thirty, maybe forty—watching, waiting to see what would happen. They stood around the perimeter of the dirt clearing—Caucasian, African American, Asian American, and Hispanic, men and women no older than twenty-four, children as young as nine, and they all wore torn white bands around their biceps.

They did not speak; it wasn't their place to get involved. Like Jhoon, they were waiting for the action to begin.

Inside the hard-packed earthen ring, Jhoon squinted and reached behind his head to tighten the frayed ends of his red bandanna. He brushed back a shock of coal-black hair that clung to his shoulder, clenched his fists, and held his ground as the three closed in.

These were the moments Jhoon lived for—the nerve-wracking seconds leading up to the first exchange. This was when he felt the most secure, shielded from those thoughts and feelings that brought him only despair. It was as if he were able to erect a wall of invincibility around him during such moments, a sort of barrier between him and the past. The tension of the fight—the jangling nerves, the electricity that surged through his arms and legs—these things were the cement that held the wall in place. Without them, the past might pour forth, the way it did at night, haunting his sleep.

Jhoon slowed his breathing, soaking in every aspect of the scene the way a painter takes in a landscape—measuring the distance between the elements, analyzing their relationship to one another—devising a strategy. He felt the familiar electricity in his legs and hands, the nerves that always accompanied him in combat. He was at his best during such moments.

A warm wind kicked up. The flames of the torches around the ring trembled.

Suddenly the big man with the huge forearms let

out a horrifying scream and charged at Jhoon like a wild animal. His cry echoed violently through the high valley walls. When he closed to within two feet of Jhoon, he raised his knee and thrust out his leg.

Jhoon stepped effortlessly—instinctively—to the side, narrowly but easily avoiding the big man's powerful front kick. Now he was in perfect position. When the man regained his balance and turned back around, he found himself face to face with the bottom of Jhoon's bare foot. Though the textbook side kick never actually touched the man, it did surprise and embarrass him.

Jhoon grinned, keeping his leg extended in front of the man's face for several seconds. He then brought the leg back down and, without looking, kicked behind him at the charging boy with the shaved head, striking him in the midsection. His body folded in half as the boy grunted and dropped to the ground, the breath knocked out of him.

The girl, whose name was Isabel, came next. She gave a loud, sustained scream, "Iyaaaaaaaa," then threw two consecutive crescent kicks—awesome strikes that whipped the air in front of Jhoon in windshield-wiperlike fashion.

The crowd gasped at the speed of her kicks. But Jhoon had already begun his counterattack, dropping to the ground and sweeping the girl's planted leg out from under her. She landed on her backside, arms splayed. The crowd around her grew silent.

The fight was over in a matter of seconds.

The exhibition was concluded, the crowd broke out in applause, and the chanting began: "Jhoon, Jhoon, Jhoon, Jhoon . . ."

As the leader of the Tribe, Jhoon now switched from fighter to advisor. He walked over to Bud, placed his hands on his hips, and gave a crooked smile. "More stomach crunches, Bud," he said. He reached down and grabbed Bud by the forearm, helping him to his feet. "You all right?"

"Fine, sir," the boy said ruefully. He faced Jhoon, gave several deep bows, then whisked himself off into the crowd.

Now Jhoon turned to Ben, the bearded man, and Isabel, asking if they too were all right. For a moment they stayed in the ring while Jhoon offered them advice and explained why their techniques had failed them. Then Jhoon stepped to the center of the ring, waved a hand in the air, and there was quiet outside the ring.

"Listen up, everyone," he shouted. "It's getting late, so I just want to remind you that the tournament is only two days away." He took a few steps forward, then looked at the others in the ring. "Only lieutenants must participate, that means Ben, Isabel, Bud, and Peter. All others may take part in preliminary matches."

"Yes, sir!" the tribe replied in unison.

"And remember," Jhoon yelled, pounding on an imaginary desk, "I'll be meeting with our spiritual leader, Mr. Jack Mann, after the tournament, so make sure everybody trains hard. I want to give Mr. Mann a good report on the Tribe's progress. We must be strong and ready to defend ourselves and the land Mr. Mann allows us to use." He paused for a moment, letting his eyes rest on various individuals in the crowd. "For now, everybody get some rest."

"Yes, sir!" the Tribe replied.

With that, everyone wandered off toward the far side of the valley. There, tents and makeshift shelters made of wood, heavy plastic, old clothing, aluminum and other discarded materials stood among the scrub oak and low-hanging trees that dotted the slight incline at the base of the valley.

In the lighted ring, Jhoon turned to Isabel and raised his eyebrows. "Has anybody seen Peter?"

Isabel swallowed hard and folded her arms over her midsection. "No, sir."

Jhoon's expression turned grim. As leader of the Tribe, anything that happened to Peter or any other member was his responsibility. It had been Peter's turn to go to the woods behind Main Street, where the best bushes and trees for picking berries were located, but it was Jhoon's work schedule that had taken him there. Gathering food was just one chore among the many that Jhoon, as leader, had assigned both to the other Tribe members and to himself. So he felt responsible. And he was worried.

In the four years since Jhoon had established the Tribe, the number of members had increased from three to forty-three, and over that time Jhoon and his four lieutenants had dealt with surprisingly few emergencies. Injuries from training were common; some were even severe. But there had been no deaths and, perhaps because word of the Tribe's hold on Talima had spread throughout the nearby region, there had been no attacks by outsiders. When drifters came through Talima, they were either recruited by the Tribe or asked in no uncertain terms to leave.

Jhoon breathed in the muggy night air. Over the western wall of the valley, patches of smoke rose and flattened, grey against the black sky. Some of the Tribe members were cooking mushroom stew, and the familiar smell wafted heavy in the air over the ring.

"Peter knows better than to walk deep into the woods," Jhoon said.

"He hates the woods," Isabel replied.

Ben scratched his beard and shook his head. "Something's not right. He should be here by now."

"Okay," Jhoon said. "I'll meet you both at the foot of the trail in about ten minutes," Jhoon said. "If Peter hasn't returned by then, we'll go look for him. Ben, bring a flashlight."

Ben looked puzzled. "Flashlight?"

Jhoon looked him squarely in the eyes. "Yes. A flashlight."

As a rule, the few flashlights the Tribe possessed were used sparingly, since they had only a handful of batteries. Consequently, flashlights, other battery-operated devices, as well as essentials like cooking utensils and matches were kept in a small storage shack. It was Jhoon's decision whether or not to use something as important as a flashlight, and up until now, he'd rarely given the order to even touch the precious few batteries. Until now there had been no reason to leave the camp at night. In fact, it had been a general rule not to. But suddenly that had changed.

Jhoon headed off to his shack, which stood above the others on the incline. For a moment he paused at the entrance to gaze down at the ring, then he quickly ducked inside.

chapter 5

Jhoon sat on the charred mattress he used as a bed and looked at himself in the cracked mirror leaning beside the door. A candle flickered beside him. He looked much older than his eighteen years. All the fighting had done that. Years of training and sparring had a way of leaving marks on a fighter, and Jhoon was no exception. His nose had been broadened by countless kicks and punches, his knuckles permanently callused, and his eyes betrayed the wariness and apprehension of men three times his eighteen years.

Sitting alone in the quiet of his small space always made Jhoon feel uneasy. Silence and inactivity were his enemy, and too much of either threatened to damage the protective wall he had worked so hard to erect, making way for the armies of doubt and dread that each night crept into his sleep. Like most survivors, Jhoon exerted almost as much energy simply trying to forget about the past, about life before the war, as he did trying to make his way in the world after it. Many did this. But for Jhoon it was particularly difficult. He fought his past and the feelings it evoked with the same intensity that he battled opponents in the ring. But the young man in the mirror was no match for these foes, and always the image of one boy's frightened face returned to haunt him—the boy Jhoon left to die.

He dipped his hands in the washbasin beside his mattress, cupped a handful of warm water, and splashed away the dirt and sweat from his face. He then returned to his mattress and looked at his meager surroundings. Jhoon's shack was made of plywood and aluminum, both of which had been taken from the basement of the Talima Post Office years ago and dragged through the woods to the valley. It was one of the more dependable shelters. Jhoon kept a crate of books in the corner of the shack, mostly books about Native Americans that he had taken from the museum in town. Several he had traded for with other Tribe members. In the corner of the shack across from the books lay a pile of dirty clothes. He had found the cracked mirror in a pile of garbage left on the road just outside Talima. There was nothing else.

Jhoon untied his bandanna, and a mane of silky dark hair fell about his shoulders. He examined the scar in the shape of a crooked "C" under his left eye.

There was a knock on the door.

"Come in."

Isabel bowed before crossing the doorway, her dark skin and prominent cheekbones bathed in shadows. "I'm sorry. Should I wait outside, sir?"

"No, it's okay. I'll just be a second." Jhoon stepped over the mattress and grabbed a green T-shirt from the pile of clothes in the corner.

Isabel looked around the room, unsure what to do. "Are we ever going to meet Jack Mann?" she asked.

Jhoon seemed surprised by the question. "Mr. Mann doesn't like to leave his home on the lake. He's something of a hermit," Jhoon said. "But someday I'd like everybody to meet him. Maybe I'll take you out to the island someday. You'd love him, Isabel. Nobody knows more about the wilderness, about the world." Jhoon pulled the shirt over his head and reached down for his bandanna. "Are you ready?"

Isabel nodded.

Ben was waiting outside. He bowed to Jhoon, and the three started up the side of the hill toward the forest.

Talima's Main Street was about a twenty-minute walk through the forest. As they entered the woods above the valley, Jhoon, Ben, and Isabel watched the trees tossing in the wind above them. They weren't concerned about Llao, the beast that was said to roam the forest. It had only been spotted in the woods north of town, up near the lake. They'd been making the trip for several years, and nothing strange or threatening had ever occurred.

Holding the flashlight out in front of him, Ben led the way down the dark trail. Now and again the moon cut through the tops of the trees, creating long, eerie shadows that moved along the ground beside them. Jhoon entertained his two disciples with exciting stories about Jack Mann, the Tribe's spiritual leader, whom only Jhoon was allowed to visit and from whom he received advice on all matters concerning the Tribe. Jhoon told Ben and Isabel the story about Jack Mann's terrifying encounter with Llao in the north woods, and how Mann escaped from Llao's clutches only by running through the great beast's woolly legs. Then the conversation turned to the martial arts, and the three discussed the upcoming tournament which Jhoon, as always, was expected to win easily.

Through a small gap in the trees, Jhoon saw the front gate, and Main Street came into view. "I'll follow the creek north along the forest," he told the others. "You two check around Main Street."

And then they emerged from the woods.

Isabel and Ben vanished over the low hill on their way to Main Street. Jhoon crept north beside the creek. He'd been on his own for about a minute when he accidentally kicked up an aluminum can hidden in a clump of weeds by his feet. The tinny sound pierced the quiet night, startling him.

He paused for a moment to regain his composure before continuing along the edge of the forest.

Around the bend he heard the soft trickling of the creek.

chapter 6

As he and Billy rested by the creek, Qwan thought about that night more than five years ago when everything started to unravel.

It was during the time when people first began to talk about the possibility of war. Qwan was in his father's tae kwon do class, standing in the front row, snapping out side kicks with the other black belts. His brother was teaching the class, wearing his favorite red bandanna, the one with the tiny figures throwing side kicks. He stood with his back to the oblong mirror, facing the students and counting off each kick in Korean.

It was the end of class. The heat and humidity had gotten more intense as the class progressed, and even though it was January, and outside the temperature was about thirty degrees, Qwan's father insisted on keeping the doors closed so that his students could get the maximum martial arts workout. The mirror that ran lengthwise in the school was foggy, and the aging wall-to-wall green mat was sticky with sweat.

When his brother finished calling out the last few kicks, he instructed the students to turn and straighten up their uniforms before bowing to the flag. His brother then left the training hall and joined his father in the front office. Qwan took his time, admiring his belt, reading his name printed in gold on the coarse black cloth. He was eight years old, the youngest black belt in the class. It had taken him only two years to earn it, beating out his brother, who had taken three years. He pulled tight the lapels on his gi top and turned toward the South Korean flag hanging on the far wall when he heard the explosion.

The sound of shattering glass echoed through the room. The noise was so loud, Qwan thought it had come from inside his brain. He raised his hands to his ears and wrinkled his face. The other students stared at each other in bewilderment, not sure of what to do. The noise had come from the front of the building. Then he remembered: His father and brother were in there.

Qwan ran into the office. The storefront window with the words "Lee's Tae Kwon Do" painted in fancy red letters had been blown to pieces, and among the broken glass at Qwan's feet lay a heavy, grey cinderblock. Neither his father nor his brother was there.

Suddenly he heard his father's voice yelling outside. Racing through the office, through the waiting room with its sneakers and shoes lined up in pairs by the doorway, Qwan burst outside into the cold, dark night.

His father, Master Lee, and his brother were standing on the sidewalk, yelling at two men who had crossed the city street and were now standing on the opposite corner.

"Why don't you go back to China where you belong," one of the men jeered, thrusting his hand into the night sky.

Qwan thought this was a strange thing to say, since he was not Chinese; his father was Korean American and his mother was Vietnamese American. He was eight years old and didn't understand why the man had said what he'd said. Master Lee turned to his sons and ordered them both inside. That's when Qwan noticed that his brother had been hit by the exploding glass. Blood trickled down his cheek from a cut under his eye—a cut in the shape of the letter "C." Master Lee was furious. Qwan had never seen him so upset.

A sharp, tinny sound rang out from down the creek and brought Qwan back to the present. Sitting up, he turned to his right and saw that Billy was sleeping. Now there was another sound. It was footsteps, and they, too, were coming from down the creek, from around the bend of the forest— approaching footsteps.

"Get up," he whispered, shaking Billy's shoulder.

Billy woke with a frightened expression. "What's going on?"

"Shh! Someone's coming." Qwan grabbed his bundle and headed for the trees, waving for Billy to follow.

They just managed to make it into the forest when the figure came into view on the other side of the creek. Qwan looked over at Billy, who was standing behind an oak about twenty feet to Qwan's left, and raised a finger to his lips. From the outline in the moonlight, Qwan could see that the figure was a man with muscular shoulders and slender hips. He watched as the shadowy figure walked slowly, pausing now and then to look into the woods or up the creek toward the log cabins. When the man was directly in front of Qwan, he stopped and turned toward the woods.

It seemed to Qwan as though the man was looking right at him, daring him to come out.

Qwan studied the man who just stood there, his back straight, his arms folded against his broad chest. He had long hair and something on his forehead. Suddenly, the figure moved a step closer, and for a moment Qwan was sure he'd been spotted. He could feel their eyes meeting, and already he began to mentally prepare himself for a fight when the figure turned and started up the creek.

In a few moments he was out of sight.

Qwan stepped cautiously over to his friend. Billy

was lying flat on the ground behind a thick bush, his face buried in his arms. As Qwan reached down to help Billy off the ground, a strange feeling surged through his body. He felt anxious, yet somehow energized. He couldn't explain it, but something was different, something had changed.

Tonight he and Billy would sleep in the woods.

chapter 7

Jhoon recognized Isabel's voice and turned around to see three figures coming toward him in the dark.

"Jhoon, we found Peter."

He had walked the length of the creek and then continued on behind the log houses on Main Street. He hadn't seen anything and was behind the Talima Indian Museum when Isabel called his name.

She now ran over to Jhoon, with Ben and Peter trailing behind.

"He was robbed, sir," Isabel said breathlessly. "Peter was robbed."

Jhoon's heart began to race. He put his hands on his hips and narrowed his eyes. "All right. Calm down. Tell me what happened."

"It's my fault, sir," Peter said glumly as he and Ben walked up. "Guess I wasn't prepared."

Jhoon examined the swelling under Peter's eye. "What happened?"

Peter glanced furtively at Isabel and Ben, then exhaled. "I was ambushed," he blurted.

Jhoon and the others remained silent, waiting for Peter to explain how this could have happened to him, a full-grown man with a lot of martial arts experience.

"I was coming out of the woods with the berries when the kid appeared out of nowhere," Peter said, staring at the ground, seemingly lost in thought. "He was amazing. The kid was amazing."

"What do you mean, amazing?" Jhoon asked, folding his arms over his chest.

Peter shook his head, smiling as if in awe of something. "I've never seen such moves, sir—except, of course, for your own. Almost knocked me out with a spinning kick. I tried to get up, but I felt pretty groggy. . . . I must have lost consciousness for a little while there on the street where Isabel and Ben found me." He gave a half smile. "The kid was quick."

Jhoon swallowed, his expression hardening. "What did he look like?"

Peter spread his legs and shook his head. "He was Asian, medium height, thin but muscular. . . ."

Jhoon felt a wave of heat course through his body. He steadied himself and took a few deep breaths. "How old was he?"

"Thirteen, maybe fifteen."

The leader of the Tribe turned and stared at the wall of forest to his left. He thought about the noise he had heard earlier by the creek. It had come from the forest, from only a few feet away from where he stood. But he had been unable to see anything through the dense stand of pines and tangled underbrush. And then, for a split second, he thought he had seen an eye staring back at him from behind a wide trunk. He had considered taking a closer look, but then the eye was gone—just a knot on a trunk, or maybe a leaf. He'd felt foolish, overeager. The way he felt now.

Only now anger was building inside him like never before, and he had to control himself, control the heat in his neck and back and the pressure in his head because he was a leader. The Tribe relied on him, so he had to stay cool and composed and sharp the way his father, Master Lee, had taught him. Besides, how much of a threat could this kid be?

"All right," Jhoon said, "let's head back to camp. We'll start our search tomorrow. If the kid is still here, we'll catch him. I promise."

He led the others back along the edge of the forest, glancing warily now and again at the woods.

Part Two
INTO THE LAKE OF A THOUSAND FACES

chapter 8

Qwan and Billy had been creeping through the dark forest on a northwesterly track for half an hour when they came upon an odd-looking shelter in a clearing.

Qwan stopped in his tracks. He raised his arm so that Billy, who had been walking several feet behind him, would also stop.

"Cool," Billy whispered over Qwan's shoulder. "Think there's anybody in it?"

Qwan took a few steps into the clearing for a better look. "Let's find out."

Billy followed close behind, pausing now and again to look over his shoulder.

Up close, the shelter resembled the Indian tepees Qwan had seen in Western movies, only this one was made from branches and bark and odd bits of fabric rather than animal skins. In the front, there was a small hanging flap that obviously served as a door.

Moonlight showered down into the clearing, making Qwan feel exposed and vulnerable. Under normal circumstances he might wait to see if anybody came or went before charging into a dwelling, but these were not normal circumstances. He had questions and wanted answers.

With Billy hovering over his shoulder, Qwan reached for the flap, cautiously pulling it up and toward him.

"Don't move," the voice from behind them said.

Qwan could feel something hard sticking in his back, something sharp. His first instinct was to kick behind him, but he wasn't sure how close the person was. Stay calm, he told himself. No reason to panic. He could hear Billy hyperventilating on his left. He started to turn toward Billy, but the thing in his back pushed a little harder.

"I could kill both of you right now. In fact, I think I will."

"Wait," Qwan said. "We didn't mean any harm. I swear. We were just looking for a place to sleep. That's all."

"Hmm—how do I know you're not part of that silly Tribe?"

"What tribe?" Billy asked. Then he felt the point in his back.

That's when Qwan made his move. Staying low to the ground, in one rapid motion he spun around and grabbed the weapon from the man's hand. He then spun around again, this time kicking out his leg, hooking the man's foot from behind and knocking him down. As the stunned assailant writhed on the ground, Qwan examined the four-foot tree branch he'd used as a weapon and smirked.

"Oh-h-h, I think you broke my back," the man moaned.

Suddenly Billy was leaning over the man. "Get up," he demanded, nudging him with his foot. "I'm gonna teach you a lesson you'll never forget."

"Cut it out," Qwan said, pushing Billy aside to examine the man.

He had a mop of curly red hair piled high on his head and hanging down over his ears like a rag doll. Qwan estimated he was in his early twenties. He was thin and bony, with freckles across his nose and cheeks. Grey warm-up pants and a dark-green sports jacket with brown patches on the elbows hung about his bony frame, and his feet were bare and caked with dirt.

"Get up," Qwan ordered.

He struggled to a sitting position, his arms draped over his knees, then began to look back and forth from Qwan to Billy.

"Get up," Qwan said more forcefully.

"I need my stick."

Billy burst out laughing. "Give me a break. You expect us to give you back your weapon?"

"It's my walking stick, genius. I'm blind."

Qwan and Billy eyed each other with stunned expressions.

The man held out his hand. "Please."

Qwan frowned, leaned over and handed the man the stick.

"How do we know he's telling the truth?" Billy muttered under his breath.

"Look at my tent, moron. Is that the work of a man with vision?"

Qwan looked back at the tent, then leaned over and grabbed the man by his forearm, lifting him off the ground. "Sorry."

"Yeah, yeah," the man groaned, pointing his stick at the tent. "Go ahead and take whatever you like. I'm used to you Tribe people. Always taking my stuff . . ."

"Look, we're not in this Tribe," Qwan said flatly. "We don't know what the Tribe is. We're not even from around here. We just want to ask a few questions."

"Not in the Tribe?" The man put a finger to his chin and nodded toward the tent. "Come inside. Let's talk."

Qwan was surprised how clean and orderly the tent was inside. Woven baskets filled with dried flowers, dried fruits, nuts, and many different berries were stacked neatly along one side wall; an old brown suitcase and a large cardboard box sat on the opposite side. A small opening at the top of the tent allowed just enough light for Qwan and Billy to see their way around. The floor was covered with a kind of patchy grey foam mattress. It was dotted with holes, and Qwan noticed a thick trail of black ants dragging a piece of an apple into one of the larger ones.

Billy sat on the mattress next to Qwan, who was positioned with his back toward the entrance of the tent, the sack of berries by his feet. "Who are you?" Qwan asked.

Perched on his suitcase, the man with the curly red hair pursed his lips and stuck out his chin. "My name is Jarrod Kapelowitz, King of Talima Forest. You can call me Jarrod."

Billy narrowed his eyes. "King of Talima Forest. Yeah, sure." He looked around, and spotting a cardboard box behind him, started groping through its contents.

Qwan pulled his knees into his chest and pressed down on the foam mattress with the tips of his fingers. "Tell me, Jarrod. Have you heard of Jack Mann?" Qwan felt a bit foolish asking this question. He didn't know why he was at all interested in Jack Mann. Nevertheless, a part of him needed to know more.

Jarrod turned his large head to one side and wrinkled his brow. "You don't know? Hmm. You really aren't from around here, are you?" His eyes wandered around the tent, stopping somewhere between Qwan and Billy. "Jack Mann is the Tribe's spiritual leader. A man of the wilderness. They say he's spent most of his life in Talima. Knows more about living in the wild than anybody on the planet.

He's something of a god to the Tribe."

"Have you ever seen him?" Qwan asked.

Jarrod gave an ironic smile.

"Oh," said Qwan, clearing his throat. "I mean, has anybody ever seen him?"

"Only a chosen few. He's the only elder in Talima, as far as I know. Lives on the island in the middle of the lake."

"What on earth is this?" Billy interrupted. He turned around to face the other two, holding a strange plastic contraption shaped like a loop with two grips at the center that came apart only with force. Around the inside of the loop were springs and coils. The word *Abs-orama* was printed on the back of the midnight-blue device. "The whole box is full of them."

Jarrod sucked in his upper lip and frowned. "Not one of my best deals. I got those in a trade with a scavenger for a pair of socks—argyle, too, or so I was told. The guy had a whole bag full of them. Said he could get a lot more. I figured I could use them for something, but as yet—"

"Do you know what it's for?" Billy asked, pulling the loop apart and placing the device over his head.

"No idea."

Qwan was growing impatient. "Can you take us to the lake?"

There was a moment of silence, then Jarrod cocked his head and let out a brief, riotous laugh. "I'm sorry," he said as he regained his breath. "It's just that nobody goes to the lake because it's too dangerous."

Qwan shifted on the mattress, his body tense. "What do you mean?"

"First of all," Jarrod explained, "to get to the lake, you have to walk about three miles north through the forest, where Llao lives. Then, you have to travel by boat another three miles, and . . ."

"What is Llao?" Billy asked, now wearing the strange contraption around his neck.

"Well," Jarrod explained, "nobody knows exactly what it is, some kind of beast, that's all. They say Jack Mann is the only one ever to face Llao, and he nearly died from it."

Billy returned the Abs-orama to its box and was now listening to every detail of Jarrod's story in rapt silence.

Qwan stretched his legs out in front of him and bent all the way over, touching his nose to his knees. "What do you know about the Tribe?" he asked.

"The Tribe is the law around here," Jarrod said with a mocking tone. His eyes darted around the tent, faster this time, and Qwan could tell that he was agitated. "We have a mutual understanding," he continued. "When I came to Talima from the north a couple of years ago, the Tribe insisted that I join, become a member, but I wasn't too thrilled about all that exercising they do." He raised a bony arm and flexed a nonexistent muscle. "As you can see, I'm not much of an athlete." Jarrod gave a crooked smile.

"Anyway, I stay away from them, and once in a while they ransack my tent and take whatever they desire." His foot began tapping the floor irritably. "The Tribe makes all the rules in Talima. For example, hunting is forbidden around here because the leader of the Tribe believes that meat slows down the body, makes you more vulnerable in fighting situations." Jarrod fingered the stubble on his chin and gave a thin smile.

Qwan unconsciously slipped a hand inside his pants pocket and felt the smooth surface of his pocket watch. He and Jarrod talked for a little while longer, Jarrod describing the Tribe in more detail, and Qwan listening intently. Billy, in the meantime, had fallen asleep in the corner, sprawled out like a tired hound.

"So I guess you're staying the night," Jarrod said with a grin. He reached down and explored the area behind his suitcase with his freckled hand. Then pulling out a lumpy blanket, he laid it out before him. "I hope there's enough space," he added, spreading the blanket on the ground and lying flat on his back.

Qwan stayed where he was, his feet drawn in to his lap, his arms resting on his knees, thinking. *Who is this Jack Mann?* Since the moment he'd heard the name spoken, questions stalked him every step of the way through Talima, stalked him like a killer. The need for sleep began to show in his eyes, but the riddle of Jack

Mann stirred in his brain and his mind forced his eyes to remain open. He had one more question. "Have you ever been to the lake?"

Jarrod got up on his elbows, a puzzled look on his face. "Once," he replied, "several years ago." He laid his head back down and folded his arms over his chest. "By accident a friend and I took the wrong trail and wound up on a cliff overlooking the lake. We climbed to the bottom and found a small boat hidden in the weeds. We were going to come back the next morning and set sail, just to see what was out there. But it was already too dark that night. He was guiding me back up the cliff when it happened."

Qwan leaned a little bit closer. "He fell?"

Jarrod nodded. "It was more than fifty feet down. If he'd hit the water he might've been okay. But he didn't."

A distant howl sliced through the quiet of the tent. Jarrod turned his head to one side, mouth agape, and gave a slight smile that might have been meant for a long-lost friend. "It's a coyote," he said softly. "They don't come around much, no animals do, but they're still out there. Somewhere."

The animal's sustained cry didn't faze Qwan. "I'll make you a deal," he said. "You take us to the lake tomorrow, and I promise you the Tribe won't bother you ever again."

Jarrod chuckled. "Yeah. How are you going to do that?"

"Trust me."

Qwan didn't know how he was going to protect Jarrod from the Tribe. He would have to figure that out later. For now, he felt a vague sense of satisfaction. He would soon get to the bottom of the mystery of Jack Mann and Talima.

The coyote howled again. When its mournful voice faded, sounds of the forest filled the tent—the clicking of crickets and the buzzing of insects. Qwan listened to the rhythms of the night, to the steady breathing of the two beside him, and then fatigue finally took him too.

chapter 9

Jhoon woke in his shack at daybreak and, as had become his custom every morning since the day he'd erected the tiny shelter in the valley, he reached across his bed for the calendar he kept by the books in the far corner. He'd found it in the Indian museum his first night in town and had brought it with him along with his few belongings to the valley. The calendar featured photos of twelve beautiful settings in and around Talima. The photo for July, which was the present month—as far as Jhoon knew—was a clearing in the forest with fat rays of light streaming down over clusters of juniper and skunk cabbage. With a pen he marked an "X" in the small box under July 17. It was hard to believe so much time had passed since he'd first come out of the desert. According to the calendar it had been more than four years. He knew because he'd been using the same calendar year after year, and the "X" he'd just marked was the fourth he'd written in the same box. Four years, he thought. It was hard to believe.

He leaned back and gazed up at the knots in the plywood ceiling. Slivers of light filtered in through the parts of the shelter that didn't meet. It was morning but already warm in the valley, and tiny beads of sweat had sprouted on Jhoon's forehead and on his bare chest and back. Soon the other members of the Tribe would rise to eat the fruits and nuts they'd collected the previous week. In the afternoon they would assemble in the dirt ring down below, and Jhoon would begin his daily tae kwon do sessions. He sat up and looked at himself in the mirror.

Four years since he'd come from the misery of the desert. But he was alive, and those who now slept peacefully in the tents below him were also alive. Those who, like him, had been brought to the desert during the days of confusion, brought to the middle of nowhere and told to wait for their loved ones, who would never return—they all had somehow survived, and with his leadership they had learned to live again. And he too had learned to live.

By forgetting about his brother.

Having left behind the desperation of the desert, he'd come to Talima on his own, running from the desolate sands and roads to the forest, hiding from his past, from what he had done. In Talima he'd found a welcome friend, a reminder of the world before everything went bad. A memory before the nightmare.

Talima was familiar to Jhoon because his parents had taken both him and his younger brother here once before the war. It had been a weekend outing, now in the distant past, when Jhoon and his family had left behind the jarring noise and fetid smells of the city and had driven three hours north through the mountains. It was spring, and together they'd spent the days hiking through the valley with its cedars and scrub oaks, camping in the forest by a creek. The woods were full of campers, and the aromas of barbecued meats and roasted marshmallows hung in the humid air.

But the Talima he returned to years later had been abandoned and stripped of mostly everything.

Everything except the memories.

He spent his first few days in Talima holed up in the Indian museum, where he slept on the polished wooden floor and read from the books no one thought to take and thought about the boy. By day he took short walks in the forest, where he discovered an abundance of berries and fruits and flowers to stave off his hunger. The water from the creek was pure and sweet, and each day he filled an ice bucket he'd found across the street in the Red Rain Tavern and kept by his side on the museum floor.

It was shortly thereafter, on a sweltering, muggy night, that he heard voices outside the cabin. Alarmed,

Qwan

he looked through a broken window and saw two figures approaching down the street. Jhoon was about to duck, to hide beneath the windowsill, hoping they would leave and that he would have the town and everything in it to himself, when suddenly one of the figures fell to the ground. Against his better judgment Jhoon left the museum to see if he could help.

The one who'd fallen was a young girl, the other a boy. They were thankful when Jhoon brought them into the museum and gave them food and water. The girl, whose name was Isabel, was suffering from malnutrition.

Isabel recovered, and she and her friend, whose name was Ben, stayed on with Jhoon at the museum.

Soon more of the desert children came— stragglers uprooted from their previous lives, looking for home and family and a modicum of comfort. Their numbers grew, and Jhoon, influenced by the books in the Indian museum, started to think of his group as a tribe. He decided that Main Street in Talima was too exposed. Not everyone they would encounter would be friendly, so he decided to take his newly found tribe to a more remote area, a place where they could be safe from whatever dangers lay ahead. There, he would train the others to defend themselves, train them the way he'd been trained—to be ready for anything.

The area Jhoon had chosen was in a nearby valley, the same valley where years earlier he'd spent an afternoon hiking with his parents and his younger brother, the one he'd abandoned, the boy he had to forget.

Four years ago.

Now Jhoon sat up and reached for a T-shirt at the foot of the bed. Enough of the past, he thought. He had more important things to consider. There was a thief in Talima. A criminal assault had been committed against one of his people, and it was his responsibility to catch the culprit and administer justice. But what justice? He would have to think about that.

He heard voices down below. The Tribe was coming to life. He looked at himself in the mirror, touched the scar under his eye. He had things to do, warriors to train.

And a thief to catch.

chapter 10

The morning sun sliced through the tops of the trees and flooded the clearing with hazy shafts of light. Qwan stood in the shade of a lanky cedar on the perimeter of the clearing, one leg extended to his side, arms folded against his chest. A symphony of chirping finches and sparrows rose in the woods around him. It felt good to work out. He hadn't been able to do so in the week it took to cross the desert, and now his legs ached with pain that was unfamiliar to his toned body. He'd been up since before the sun, practicing kicks mostly—front kicks and side kicks and axe kicks and crescent kicks and his personal favorite, the spinning hook kick, in which he spun around on his front foot while cocking his back leg and whipping it out at the imagined target. It was his favorite kick, and sometimes he jumped when he threw it to get more height, the way he had the night before against the African American man in the street.

He felt the muscles in his leg burning. He'd kept it extended in the air now for close to five minutes. This was the last and most grueling part of his workout, holding the leg out in front, to the side, and behind, each for five minutes. Next he would do the same with the other leg. Sweat streamed down his chest and arms, and he lowered his leg with a grunt just as Jarrod emerged from the tent.

"Good morning," Jarrod said, stepping into the clearing with the aid of his walking stick. In his free hand he held a small handmade basket filled with dark berries. "Try some of these," he offered, holding out the basket. "They're much tastier than the ones you brought."

Qwan dipped his hand in the basket. Jarrod was right, the berries were better—sweeter, too. He grabbed a few more from the basket and rested his eyes on Jarrod. In the light of day he looked even more frail and weak than he had the night before. His knotty, curly red hair was pushed up on one side, the side he had slept on, and a cowlick sprouted up like a weed on the very top of his head. He wore the sweatpants from the night before, a purple tank top that exposed toothpick arms covered with freckles, and his toes stuck out of his sandals by nearly two inches.

But what really got Qwan's attention were his eyes. They were scarred and watering, which he hadn't noticed in the darkness the previous night. Jarrod had not been blind at birth. Qwan had seen similar scars before. They were scars caused by the flash.

"So, where do you come from?" Jarrod asked, taking a seat on the ground.

Qwan raised his other leg straight out to the side. "The desert."

"Not surprised. Mostly everybody alive does. Except for me. I'm from the north." He popped a few berries into his mouth. "Got any brothers or sisters?"

"No," Qwan answered sternly. "No family."

Billy then stuck his head out the flap of the tent, his weary eyes squinting in the brilliant sunlight. "You guys up already?" he croaked, his voice congested with sleep. "Hey, Qwan. Wait for me, man. I'm gonna work out, too."

Qwan's leg gave a slight quiver, the muscles in his thigh beginning to pull. He looked down at Jarrod sitting on the ground before him. "We should leave for the lake in a few hours," he said, "just before sundown when it cools off."

Jarrod nodded. "Fine with me."

Then Qwan looked at Billy. "All right then. Get your leg up."

As Billy stretched, then lifted his right leg while supporting himself on a wobbly left leg, Qwan felt his own leg giving way. But he fought back, lifting it even higher, until he could no longer take the pain. Then he took a few deep breaths and started again, this time with Billy.

chapter 11

Later that same day, Jhoon was standing in front of his class, conducting the second of his two daily tae kwon do sessions. He clasped his hands around his back and stared up at the wall of forest towering over the eastern side of the valley. It was already late afternoon, the sun baking the valley floor, and the session was nearing an end.

"Keep it up, Peter. Ten more seconds. Keep it up," Jhoon said. His expression was intense. He stood practically right on top of his student.

In the stifling heat, Peter stood in the first of six rows of students that covered the entire dirt ring in the center of the valley. His outstretched leg spasmed. He grunted and grimaced, sweat pouring down his forehead, his muscles beginning to tighten and contract. Despite his effort, he could see through narrowed eyes that his leg was beginning to drop. When it finally touched the ground, he bent over and grabbed his aching knee, sucking both lips into his mouth and shaking his head, disgusted.

"Get down and give me fifty stomach crunches," Jhoon said grimly.

The others in the first row looked on with uneasy faces. So far class had been more grueling than usual. It was clear to all that something was bothering Jhoon.

"All right," Jhoon yelled, stepping back and addressing the whole class. "Put 'em down." He swiveled his hips and wiped sweat rolling down his neck. "Now the other leg."

Peter finished his crunches and rejoined the line. He lifted his right leg straight ahead, parallel with the ground. Jhoon sidled over to him, watching like a hawk. Gritting his teeth, Peter looked away from Jhoon. The pain was now in both legs, a sharp, stabbing pain.

"Keep it up, Peter." Jhoon got down in a squat position and looked up at his student, a vague smile crossing his lips. "Another minute, that's all."

Peter could take it no more.

"What's your problem, man?" Peter's voice was loud and thick with rage. He lowered his leg and took a step in Jhoon's direction. "You know I'm hurting. What's your problem?"

Slowly, with patience and calm and absolute control, Jhoon rose up before his student and took one step backward, the line of his mouth curled slightly up on one side. He then settled into a side stance with his hands stretched out before him. "Bring it on," he challenged Peter.

Suddenly the class fell out of line, rushing to the front and forming a tight circle around the combatants. Isabel stepped forward, her hands pressed firmly against her hips. While the rest of the students began yelling and chanting, she alone remained silent.

"All right," Peter said. "You want a fight? You got it."

They circled cautiously, each making sure to keep the same distance between himself and the other. Then Peter moved forward and threw a quick jab at Jhoon's face. The punch didn't land, but it got Jhoon's attention. He blew a shock of hair out of his eyes and gave a feint with both hands, causing Peter to flinch.

From a few feet away, Ben pumped a fist in the air and began to chant, "Jhoon, Jhoon, Jhoon, Jhoon." Isabel glared at him. She clamped her teeth down on her fist and withdrew a few feet into the crowd. But already Ben had gotten the rest of the class to join him, their cheers and catcalls reaching a fevered pitch.

Rhythm was everything, and Jhoon knew well the importance of rhythm in combat. An opponent's every move—the lifting of a knee, a sudden shifting of the eyes, the speeding up or slowing down in the hands or feet—all signaled intent and direction. They were all part of a rhythm, and every fighter had his or her own symphony of twitches and jerks and sequences within sequences that a skilled fighter could pick out, note, and remember. Jhoon was such a fighter. He watched the way Peter moved his feet and hands and head and, most importantly, his eyes, and the rhythm told him what to do and when to do it, which kick or punch to throw, where to move. Rhythm was everything.

After a few moments, Jhoon had memorized every note—every beat—of Peter's rhythm. He wrenched forward, and Peter jerked back, dropping his hands a few inches. Jhoon suddenly stomped his foot on the ground, and again Peter flinched. Then Jhoon pulled his arm into his chest and lurched forward with all his momentum, uncoiling a powerful back fist that struck Peter in the mouth, opening a small but deep cut on his upper lip.

He didn't stop there.

Peter raised a hand to his mouth to check the extent of the damage when Jhoon struck again, this time with his feet. He slid forward, raised his left knee almost level with his head, and snapped out a series of punishing round-house kicks that landed on the spot where Peter had been struck the night before. One after another the kicks came, and all the while Jhoon never lowered his kicking foot to the ground.

Ben and the crowd roared their approval, arms raised over their heads.

Isabel hurried into the ring and ran between the two fighters. "Enough!" she screamed as Peter and Jhoon struggled to get at each other over her extended arms.

Jhoon, too, had lost himself. Despite his belief in the importance of composure, which he'd been taught all throughout his martial arts training, he'd lost himself in the heat of the moment, and he could do nothing to stop the rage that flowed through his arms and legs. He could hear himself breathing, sucking in irregular gulps of air. He knew he was out of control but for some reason did nothing to stop it. He wanted just one more score, wanted to feel once more his hand or foot smashing against another's flesh.

It was by accident that it was Isabel he struck.

He hadn't even realized she had come between them when the punch struck the side of her head just below her temple. It was Peter's expression, a look of horror and dismay, which first alerted Jhoon that something terrible had happened.

In front of the stunned crowd, Isabel's body fell limply to the earthen floor. And then Jhoon came back to the present. He kneeled by Isabel's side and grabbed her arm while the others looked on in silence.

chapter 12

Qwan, Billy, and Jarrod hiked down a cramped path surrounded by limbless pines and lush undergrowth. They'd left Jarrod's tent late in the afternoon, after taking a long nap during the hottest part of the day. The sun was in front of them, level with the forest, as they followed the path to the lake on a northwesterly tract.

Jarrod's hand was clamped on Qwan's shoulder as he walked a step behind him. In his other hand he held his walking stick. Billy brought up the rear.

Qwan soon noticed that the forest was changing as they walked deeper into the woods. There were no longer any flowers by the side of the trail, and the trees had gnarled and twisted trunks, with white bark and long, spindly weeds growing at their feet. Qwan thought they looked deformed and grotesque. He'd never seen trees like these. Even the birds shied away from this part of the forest. Their songs could only be heard from a distance. It was eerie, he thought, too eerie.

The deeper into the woods they went, the quieter Billy and Jarrod became. If it hadn't been for Jarrod's tenacious grip on his shoulder, Qwan might have thought his friends had vanished.

Jack Mann.

The name resonated in Qwan's brain. But he still couldn't place it, and now a sense of desperation and foolishness threatened to sabotage his determination to get to the lake. He wasn't sure their trip would lead to anything, and the thought of going to some out-of-the-way lake just on a vague hunch seemed to be a bit foolish. But he had to learn the truth about Jack Mann.

Still the trip was reckless, and he had to think of Billy. It wasn't as though he felt responsible for bringing Billy along. That was Billy's choice—just like it had been Billy's choice to follow Qwan everywhere he went since the time they first met in the desert several years ago. Qwan remembered the day vividly.

He had been living alone at an abandoned restaurant along a sun-bleached two-lane highway, having spent the previous weeks battling the sickness that had taken the lives of the adults in the shelter. Sleeping in a booth in the back of the restaurant one night, his bundle of clothes and assorted other things on the floor, Qwan heard someone snooping around.

He watched as a thin, blond-haired boy reached down to steal his bundle. Then, just as the boy was about to take off with it, Qwan sat up, jumped out of the booth, and whipped his leg around in an arcing motion, coming only inches from the boy's nose. Backing up, the boy put out his hands as if to signal his defeat, then retreated, without uttering a word.

The next morning, Qwan was about to leave the restaurant to find some food when he found the boy sleeping on the pavement next to the twin gas pumps out front.

For days the boy hung around, keeping to himself, watching Qwan come and go. Then one day he approached Qwan in front of the restaurant. "Please," he said, "teach me what you know. I just want to learn to protect myself."

Billy had been with him ever since.

Qwan swatted a mosquito on his neck. A second later he slapped another of the pests on his arm, then another, this time on the back of his neck. He heard Jarrod and Billy doing the same behind him. He looked off the trail to his left, saw a narrow creek beyond the thickening brush, and grinned, shaking his head. Qwan hated mosquitos.

"How far from here?" Billy's voice shattered the silence.

Tightening his grip on Qwan's shoulder, Jarrod pulled to a stop and began moving his head back and forth in the dimming light. "When we reach 'the rock,' it's about another fifteen minutes."

"What rock?" Billy wanted to know, coming up tight on Jarrod's back. His eyes were wide with uncertainty.

Qwan could tell by the sound of Billy's voice that he was growing nervous, and if Billy held true to form he would probably babble the rest of the way.

"You'll see it," Jarrod answered, pointing his walking stick. "It stands in the middle of the trail. Have to walk around it. In fact," he continued, "it's near the spot where Llao is said to hunt."

Billy laughed—a forced laugh—and again came up around the side of the other two. "You don't actually believe that story, do you?"

Jarrod shrugged. "I guess anything's possible. You know, since the war."

chapter 13

In the valley, the late afternoon sun had already begun its slow descent over the western wall. The heat hung heavy in the air, sticky like glue. Dripping with sweat, Jhoon dipped his cup into a bucket of water and passed it over to Isabel. The searing heat filled his head with a growing tension that made it difficult for him to move and to think.

They were sitting across from one another in Isabel's tent. Jhoon felt depressed and remorseful as he looked at Isabel sitting on several layers of blankets that she used as a bed, her arms resting on her knees, her hands clasped. There was a slight swelling on the side of her head where he had struck her.

"It was an accident, sir," Isabel said. "Really, I'm fine."

Jhoon hadn't known what to say to her from the moment he'd picked her up off the dirt floor of the ring. As it happened, Isabel never lost consciousness; the blow merely stunned her. But it gave everybody a scare. After apologizing to Peter, Jhoon immediately called off the rest of the class, and with Ben's help he carried Isabel to her tent. There she rested for a time before Jhoon came back to check on her.

"I don't know what got into me," he said softly, glancing tentatively in her direction. "I guess everything that happened last night . . ."

"You don't have to explain." Isabel smiled and looked away. "As long as I can go along with Ben and Peter."

Jhoon looked confused. "What do you mean?"

"To look for the thief."

He nodded back at Isabel and reached for another cup of water. In all the confusion, Jhoon had forgotten all about sending out a party to look for the thief. After the incident in the ring, everybody had gone to their tents without discussion as Jhoon had ordered. But now he realized there might be another reason why he'd forgotten about it. Part of him felt ambivalent about the matter. He almost wanted to call the whole thing off. They were only berries, and whoever stole them was obviously alone and posed little threat to the Tribe. Besides, tomorrow was the monthly tournament, the event everybody looked forward to, and Jhoon didn't want to be disturbed by outsiders.

But the Tribe needed to know stealing wouldn't be tolerated. For that reason he would send his lieutenants out to have a look around the area, even though he seriously doubted they would find anything.

He stood up and dug his hands into his pockets. "Sure you're up to it?" he asked softly.

"Yeah," Isabel replied, laying her legs straight out and stretching her back all the way forward so that her nose reached to her knees. "I'm fine, really."

Jhoon smiled and backed up toward the opening in the tent. "All right," he said. "When you're ready, go get Ben and Peter, and have Ben take a flashlight. It'll be dark soon."

"Yes, sir." Isabel got to her feet and slipped through the plastic opening of the tent.

"And don't be back too late," he called from outside. "You've got a tournament tomorrow."

chapter 14

The dying rays of sunlight flitted in and out from behind the trees as Qwan and the others made their way down the darkening path. There had been silence for the last few minutes, and Qwan's mind had begun to wander, drifting back to a night when it was also quiet, and when the lights that flitted by came from traffic on a highway.

It was several weeks after the incident at his father's tae kwon do school, and Qwan was on a bus, looking out the window at the lights above the highway, watching them glide by, slow and ominous, like searchlights. The bus he rode in was full, mostly with children and young adults, and everyone was quiet, morbidly quiet.

His brother sat beside him, on the aisle. They said nothing to one another; they didn't have to. Both were thinking the same thoughts, feeling the same feelings—

fear, uncertainty, disbelief—but the depth of their thoughts went beyond words, so neither boy spoke. They just looked out the window at the passing lights.

Earlier that same day Qwan had been in his family's apartment in the city, sitting next to his brother at the kitchen table and drinking from a can of soda. Suddenly their mother came storming in from her bedroom down the hall. She'd been talking on the videophone, and Qwan had heard her voice rising a few times during the conversation, which was something she rarely did. He was only eight years old, but he knew something was terribly wrong because his mother never raised her voice. She sat down at the kitchen table beside him and tried her best to smile, but Qwan knew she was upset. Her eyes were red and swollen, and in one corner he saw a dried streak where a tear had fallen.

She told them they would have to go away for a while, and soon she and their dad would come up north and pick them up. Jhoon got up from the table and went to his room. Their mother didn't say anything else; she didn't have to. Qwan knew what was going on. He had been hearing about the possibility of war. That's all anybody had been talking about, including his parents, although they tried to do it when he and his brother were out of earshot. Before he left the table he told his mother that it was okay, and that he knew they would come back for him.

Later, when he went to his bedroom to pack his things, he walked by his parents' room and saw them sitting on the foot of their bed watching the wall viewer. He couldn't make out what the woman on the screen was saying, but he knew that she was the President, and whatever she said hit his parents pretty hard. His mother's hands shot up to her mouth. Dad just stared straight ahead.

That night Qwan's mother and father took him and his brother to the bus station downtown, and as he followed his brother up the steps of the bus, he turned around and waved to his parents, who were shivering on the sidewalk. That was the last time Qwan saw his parents.

On the bus to the desert no one spoke a word. Qwan looked out the window at the lights over the highway, studying each one as it passed, and hoping he would see his parents again.

It was nearly dark when Qwan saw "the rock." He reached into his pants pocket for his watch, curious about how long it had taken them to get here from Jarrod's tent, but the watch was gone. Quickly he thrust his hand into his other pocket. Had it fallen out somewhere along the way? Had he left it back at Jarrod's tent? It was the only linkage he allowed himself to the past. It had to be there. If it had fallen out on the trail, the watch would be next to impossible to find. For now, though, there was nothing he could do.

Qwan

Qwan turned his attention to "the rock," which was actually a huge boulder, standing some six feet high. Up close it looked like an enormous potato. It had a greyish-brown hue, with black striations and large holes like pock marks throughout. Sickly yellow weeds sprouted out from beneath the boulder, curling themselves up and around the base of it like wispy fingers.

"The rock" blocked the entire path and extended several feet into the brush on either side. Reaching around Jarrod's back, Qwan squeezed between it and the shrubbery to the other side of the trail. Billy followed behind them.

"About fifteen minutes from here," Jarrod said, tightening his grip on Qwan's shoulder.

That's when they heard the sound.

It came from the thick brush off to the right, a sound like a rake combing through grass. Only louder. Billy's mouth hung wide open. Jarrod remained perfectly still, craning his neck, the lines on his forehead creased.

Qwan, too, froze. He hadn't believed the story about Llao when Jarrod had mentioned it the day before. Rumors about all sorts of monsters and mutants had been common in the desert, yet Qwan had never seen any of them. But that didn't mean it wasn't a possibility. As Jarrod had said, anything was possible.

He leaned into the branches and leaves, quietly sweeping them aside to get a better look. He could feel

Billy's breath on his neck. Both peered into the dark mix of trunks and shrubs and low rock formations, and at the same time they saw something like arms, massive arms, black against the moonlit sky, raised as high as the tallest trees. Billy gasped, spun around, and started running down the trail.

"Is it Llao?" Jarrod asked. But Qwan merely grabbed Jarrod and raced after Billy.

They'd been running since the moment they saw the thing in the woods, scarcely exchanging a word, Billy in the lead, Qwan and Jarrod several steps behind, when they finally reached the crest overlooking the lake.

Billy skipped to a stop, then turned to face the others. "There," he cried, catching his breath, one arm pointing toward the lake. "There it is!"

Qwan and Jarrod stepped closer to the edge. "Finally," Qwan breathed, his thoughts filled with Jack Mann.

But Billy was still thinking about Llao. He turned back toward the path, trembling. "We probably imagined the whole thing. Don't you think, Qwan? Just a shadow or something, right?"

"Well," Jarrod replied, "if it was Llao, he didn't come after us. Which either means the creature's not as bad as everyone says, or it wasn't hungry."

Billy glared at Jarrod, then glanced once more back down the gloomy trail.

Qwan didn't know what he'd seen in the woods. He thought he'd seen something. But the dark often played tricks on the eyes, and Jarrod was right: if there was something out there, it certainly wasn't interested in them. Or so it had seemed.

Now the lake stretched before him. He stepped a few feet closer to the edge of the cliff and got down in a squat position.

Somber. That's the word that came to his mind when he gazed over the cliff and felt the whole of the lake overtake him, rush through him. The full moon overhead beamed down an expanse of silver light that rolled out over the lake as far as he could see. He looked north and then south. The rugged cliff and the lake below seemed to go on forever. It was huge, like an ocean. But still, with no waves. Somber.

Qwan looked down the steep slope at the narrow, rugged shoreline and the tranquil black water. He judged the drop to be about fifty feet, almost straight down, with immense black rocks that shone like glass lining the way. Small plants and gnarled weeds grew between the rocks and along the side of the cliff.

Qwan got to his feet, wiped dirt from his hands and turned to the other two. He looked at Jarrod. "Are you sure you can do this?"

"Sure," Jarrod said, swinging his arms, his head cocked to the side. "I did it before; I can do it again." Then Jarrod tossed his walking stick over the side and reached out for Qwan.

Qwan then turned to Billy. "You ready?"

Billy didn't answer at first. He looked nervously back and forth from the cliff to the trail behind him. "Yeah," he said, forcing a smile. "I'm ready."

Qwan got behind Jarrod and carefully led him down the cliff, keeping an eye on his feet and legs in case Jarrod lost his footing or couldn't place his step.

Halfway down the cliff Qwan looked up and noticed that Billy had stopped climbing. His head was turned to the side and pressed up against the cliff wall, and his hands clung to the rocks on either side. Qwan could see that he was breathing rapidly. "What's wrong?" Qwan yelled.

Billy looked down at Qwan and Jarrod but he didn't speak.

"Don't look down," Qwan advised. "You'll be all right. Just don't look down."

Billy's chest and back heaved. "I can't."

"Billy," Qwan said, wiping the sweat from his forehead onto his shoulder, "which do you think is more dangerous—climbing another few feet down this cliff, or staying up there, alone, near the forest?"

Billy glanced quickly up, then looked slowly down. As if his hands and feet had suddenly come to life, he began moving hurriedly toward Qwan and Jarrod, catching up to them in a matter of seconds.

"Come on," he breathed. "I'm with you."

When they reached the bottom of the cliff, making their way along the narrow shoreline under the moonlight, the mosquitos came at them in thick swarms. "Crap," Billy said in a sneering voice, slapping one dead on his cheek.

Qwan tried his best to ignore the insects, but they were too persistent, jabbing their needle-like beaks into his arms, face, and neck. "Darn," he groaned, craning his neck to track the descent of the pesty creatures. The shoreline extended about fifty feet to the edge of the water and was covered mainly with dirt and rocks and yellowish grass. He walked out to the water, swatting clouds of mosquitos, and looked far out on the lake.

"Here it is!" Jarrod's voice was excited.

Qwan and Billy joined him by the base of the cliff, where Jarrod had pulled a rowboat out from the brush. The boat was made of a dark blue plastic and had two crosspieces, making three seats. They dragged it out to waist-deep water and one by one hopped over the side. Qwan offered to help Jarrod into the boat, but he refused, grunting and snorting and struggling before he finally pulled himself in. "Straight ahead," Jarrod said. "It's supposed to be straight out, about a mile."

Qwan labored to see in the dark, trying to imagine the island way out in the middle of the lake. He grabbed the oars from the muddy floor and began to row, facing Jarrod in the middle seat, his back to the unknown.

chapter 15

Peter and Isabel entered the clearing from the dark woods and approached the tent with caution, listening to hear if anyone was inside, then nodding to one another when they thought it was safe to go in. They'd been out looking for the thief for more than an hour and as yet had found nothing.

Peter raised the flap and looked in. "Nobody here," he said. "Should we have a look around?"

"Can't hurt to look," Isabel replied, pointing the flashlight into the dark tent and ducking inside.

Peter was right behind her. "I wonder where our friend Jarrod is?" he asked, looking inside a cardboard box.

Beaming the flashlight on the baskets in the far corner, Isabel removed the lid on the top basket and looked inside. "Uhm, dried apples," she said, replacing the lid and turning the flashlight on the old suitcase.

"Nothing here," Peter said, pushing through the flap. He was a few feet outside the tent when something on the ground caught his eye. "Hey, shine the light over here for a second."

Isabel emerged from the tent and pointed the beam of her light at the spot.

"Down here," Peter said, crouching on the ground. He picked something up and examined it in his hand.

"What is it?" Isabel asked.

Peter held out his hand. The object was a black pocket watch. "I'm sure Jhoon will be happy to see another piece of hardware added to the collection." Peter dangled the watch in the stream of light for Isabel to see.

She leaned foward. "A yin-yang symbol. Interesting." She gave Peter a sidelong glance. "But do you really think we should take it?"

"I don't think our old friend Jarrod bought it at the corner store either," Peter remarked. "You know the rules, finders keepers . . ."

Peter shoved the watch in his pocket. Ben would be waiting for them back on Main Street. They jogged across the clearing and headed down the trail, passing a fallen log on their right, behind which Qwan had hidden his and Billy's bundles as well as what was left of Peter's sack of berries.

chapter 16

Qwan heard a splash off the right side of the boat.
"What was that?" Billy whispered.

Even in the dark Qwan saw the ripples on the black surface of the lake. "Probably a trout," he guessed, resting his arms for a few seconds before resuming his rowing.

Jarrod reached down and twirled a finger in the muddy water on the bottom of the boat. "They say if you look long and hard into the depths of the lake, you will see a thousand sorrowful faces staring back up at you, the faces of the dead. Their arms rising toward you, reaching up as if in one desperate—"

"Cut it out," Billy snapped.

"Well," Jarrod said, "that's what they say."

A moment later, Qwan saw Billy's mouth suddenly open wide, and he turned in his seat to see what Billy was seeing.

It was the island, a couple hundred yards away, a

dark silhouette against the moonlit sky. As it came into view, Qwan saw that it was not very big, no bigger than a football field, and fairly low to the ground.

A light mist rose from the shoreline, giving the island an isolated look, as if it had nothing to do with its surroundings.

"What's it look like?" Jarrod asked.

Billy swallowed and inched forward in the boat. "Creepy," he said. "Real creepy."

Qwan rowed close to the shoreline, then helped Jarrod out into knee-deep water. As he pulled the boat onto the rugged shore, Qwan noticed the wooded area beyond the shore was replete with black and dark-red rock formations. Some rose as high as ten feet, splitting off into sharp pinnacles that stood alongside scraggly hemlocks and shrubbery. It looked as if the tiny island had been the result of a volcanic explosion, and Qwan couldn't imagine that anyone actually lived within its dense landscape. He stood on the shore with his thumbs hooked in his pants pockets, looking around in the dark.

"Uh, guys," Jarrod said. "I don't want to spook you or anything, but I just heard something move." He was facing the dense wall of foliage and rock, his head cocked.

Qwan and Billy stood beside Jarrod, listening to the woods around them.

"It came from over there." Jarrod pointed his

walking stick toward a stand of thick green bushes fronting the shoreline.

Qwan sidled up to take a look, the other two following closely behind. He peered into the dark brush but could hardly see a thing. The island was so wild and overgrown and dark that it was virtually impossible to distinguish one leaf or branch from another. He was about to turn back when he saw something streaking through the vegetation off to his right. It was white, perhaps somebody's shirt. He moved a few feet down the shoreline and stared at the spot in the brush where he'd seen the movement. There was nothing, but he did see a small trail that led into the woods several feet down from where he stood.

He turned around to face the others. "Jarrod, you stay and guard the boat," Qwan said. "Billy, you come with me."

With Billy by his side, Qwan squeezed into the cramped trail.

As they continued down the dark trail, the landscape began to thin out, making their passage easier. Moonlight illuminated their way, and Qwan could see a clearing about twenty feet ahead and what looked like a small cabin off to one side.

He stopped in his tracks.

"What is it?" Billy asked.

"Looks like an old cabin." Qwan scanned the clearing. A large rock formation stretched around the dwelling and continued in a snaking fashion down a slight incline beyond, where the vegetation thickened.

The cabin was made of thin logs, with an opening like a window in the side facing Qwan, and no door. It was tiny, and on the roof were several spaces where logs had fallen off and now lay in the clearing beside the cabin.

"Doesn't look like anybody's in there," Qwan whispered.

"How do ya know?" Billy asked. "You said you saw somebody back there. How do ya know they're not in there now?"

"Stay here," Qwan said. "I'm going to check it out."

"Are you sure it's safe?" Billy asked, holding Qwan by the arm.

Qwan pulled away from Billy and darted across the clearing, looking from side to side. When he reached the cabin, he flattened his chest and arms against the logs and slowly inched toward the window, pausing to look back at Billy, who hadn't moved an inch. Then he looked in the window.

There was nobody inside, so Qwan stepped inside the dark room.

A desk and chair made of logs faced the window from the far corner of the cabin, and along the opposite wall sat a long, flat slab of polished black rock. Several sheets of paper were spread out over the slab, and among them Qwan found an old photograph of a young man wearing an open army shirt. He held it up by the window where there was some light.

The man's skin was streaked with red dust, and the same dust hung in the air around him, giving the whole photo a brown tint. On the back of the photo someone had written in blue ink: "Quang Tri Province, South Vietnam, 1969." Next to the photo was a set of army ID dog tags. Qwan read the name, and it all came back to him.

It was an incident that occurred the weekend he and his family visited Talima, before the war. Qwan had done more than just hike through the woods and visit shops on Main Street. He just hadn't remembered it until now. He'd shut the memory out because it had frightened him.

It was their first night of the vacation, and Qwan's parents had gone to sleep in their tent while he and Jhoon stayed up talking in their own tent. Instead of going right to sleep, they decided to take a flashlight and go for a walk along the creek, despite their father's warning not to leave the tent after dark.

They walked north along the creek for a good mile, laughing and sparring with one another along the way. It was warm that night, and at one point both boys kneeled over the creek to drink the cool water. That's when Qwan felt the barrel of a rifle go into his back and heard a man command him to turn around, slow.

Qwan and his brother obeyed, and turning around they saw that the man holding the rifle wore an old army fatigue jacket. He was old, with deep wrinkles in his forehead, long, stringy hair, and a long yellow-grey beard. The boys stood motionless. And finally the man, realizing they weren't a threat, lowered his rifle and sat down on the ground next to them.

He told Qwan and his brother that they shouldn't be out in the woods all alone, that the woods were too wild and dangerous for civilized people, let alone young kids. He said he'd been living in the wilderness for many years. It was a place he could trust, where he felt safe. For a long while he talked about the woods and the lake and the animals, all of which he considered his family. Qwan listened nervously, keeping an eye on the gun by the man's side. Jhoon seemed enthralled by the man's talk, hanging on to his every word. At one point the old man's face hardened, and he looked grimly down at the dirt and weeds by his feet. "War will come soon," he said in a raspy voice. He grabbed one of the dog tags hanging from his neck and placed it between his blackened teeth, biting down, then spitting out the metal tag. "I've known war," he said, pulling at his beard with long, yellow fingernails. "My younger brother and I both served in Vietnam. Saw a lot of bad things over there, but at least I came back." He stared at Qwan. "They never found my brother."

Qwan swallowed and turned away from the old

man's unblinking eyes. "War will come soon," the man repeated. Then he announced he was tired, asked for the boys' names, shook their hands, and introduced himself before he got up off the ground to leave. Almost as suddenly as he'd appeared, he was gone, vanishing into the night, his rifle by his side. His name was Jack Mann.

Qwan laid Jack Mann's dog tags back on the desk in the cabin and squinted in the darkness. His mind reeled.

What did it mean? He tried to put everything in perspective, make sense of the situation. But he couldn't focus his thoughts.

Then he noticed a book on the floor beside the desk. He picked it up and again walked over to the doorway for light. The book was called *The Myth of Llao and Other Tyee Legends*, and sticking out of it, marking a page, was a worn piece of fabric. He pulled it out and felt the blood rush out of his legs. It was a tattered red bandanna, with prints of little men throwing side kicks.

One of Jhoon's bandannas.

He felt a rage building from deep inside him. Now it all made sense: Jack Mann, Llao, the Tribe, martial arts—and Jhoon.

He was here, in Talima.

He pictured his brother's face looking at him from

inside that church, imagined him walking out the door.

And never returning.

That's OK, brother, Qwan thought. *Because I'm coming to you, and this time I'm leaving you on the ground.* He threw the book back onto the floor.

Part Three
INTO THE RING

chapter 17

Jhoon was lying down on his mattress, wondering what had happened to Ben, Isabel, and Peter, when he heard the knock.

"Who is it?"

"It's us." Isabel's voice was upbeat.

"Come in." Isabel and Peter ducked inside the shack. "Where's Ben?" Jhoon asked.

"Asleep," Peter replied, taking a seat on the floor. "Wants to be fresh for the tournament tomorrow."

Jhoon examined the swelling on the side of Isabel's head, considered mentioning it, then decided to move on. "So, did you find the thief?"

Isabel stood by the door with her arms folded. "Nope," she replied. "We checked from Main Street all the way to the woods up near Jarrod's place. Didn't see a thing. He must have left town the same night he came."

Jhoon locked his hands around the back of his

head, leaned back, and yawned. It was a great relief that the whole matter had come to a close. Now he could look forward to fighting tomorrow in the tournament. He would win, reassert his power, and everything would go back to normal in Talima. For the first time in several days his mind was at ease.

"Oh," Peter said, reaching into his pocket. "I did find this outside Jarrod's tent." He leaned across the mattress and handed the watch to Jhoon.

Jhoon's heart turned to ice. It was the watch he'd given his brother.

Qwan was alive.

The protective wall Jhoon had worked so hard to erect since that night in the church suddenly shattered into tiny pieces. He dropped the watch to the floor and looked down, glowering at it, as if this simple timepiece were to blame for bringing the past back to him.

Suddenly everything was painfully clear. The thief with the martial arts skills . . . an Asian boy . . .

And now the watch.

Peter and Isabel were looking at Jhoon with tilted heads, speaking to him, gesturing. But he couldn't hear them. Not over the sound of the crumbling wall.

"Please leave," he said mournfully, turning his back as Ben and Isabel left the shack. "There'll be no tournament tomorrow," he added.

"Sir?" Peter asked, not sure what Jhoon had said.

"Leave!" Jhoon said, his voice forceful now.

Qwan

As the sounds of Isabel's and Peter's footsteps faded away, images came back to him, and he could no longer resist them, could no longer hide from their truth. There was Qwan's face covered with sweat, there was the look in his eyes just before Jhoon turned his back on him.

It was during the chaotic first months after the war when the food in the shelters ran out, and most of the desert children left to find their own provisions in order to survive. They walked in the cool of night to the nearest towns, wandering up and down the streets and taking whatever they could find.

New and awful diseases came in the wake of the war, and rumors began to spread that the sickness could be transmitted through the air. Fear and hate added to the turmoil, and what was once a unified community struggling to survive soon split up into small groups that looked out only for themselves.

Jhoon and Qwan were alone in this chaos. They left the shelter and journeyed west through abandoned roads until they'd come to a small deserted town nestled in a valley. There, they took refuge in the back of a church, scouring the shops and homes during the day and staying close by at night. Sometimes bands of scavengers came through the town, and when they came into the church, Jhoon and Qwan fought them off with their hands and feet.

Life was difficult, but they were surviving, living off whatever they could forage in the nearby houses and stores. They'd felt lucky to be alive, lucky to have been spared the sickness they'd heard about in the shelter. They even talked about trying to make their way back home. This even though they both feared what they might find.

Then one night, after Qwan had already gone to sleep in the small office in the back of the church, Jhoon was settling into his sleeping bag when he looked over at his brother and noticed sweat dripping down his face and chest. Jhoon's whole body froze. He got up, walked over to the boy, and saw large red splotches on his arms and neck.

His mind was swimming in fear. He'd heard that the sickness was contagious. Stories about how fast the disease took its victims had been legion in the shelter, and he'd seen evidence of it himself. Jhoon sat against the opposite wall of the room, trembling and thinking, desperately trying to find an answer, when his father's words came back to him.

They were at the bus station, on the last night. Jhoon's father, Master Lee, had taken Jhoon aside while Mrs. Lee talked to Qwan farther down the platform.

"You are the oldest," Master Lee had said. "With age comes privilege but also responsibility. I don't want your brother to know this, and I've never said it to your mother, but things are very bad." His eyes welled with tears. "You must take care of your little brother. Do everything you can to keep him safe." Master Lee hugged his oldest son. "But there's something else you must promise me," he said. "The family must survive. Whatever you do, make sure one of you stays alive. The family must live on. If you must die to save your brother, then you must give yourself for him. If you must sacrifice your brother to save yourself, do it. I cannot bear the thought of our family ending because of this insane war. Make sure that at least one of you survives."

The words resonated in Jhoon's brain as he sat in the little office in the back of the church and cried, cried as he looked over at his brother, who was sweating and shaking.

That same night, he rolled his things into a bundle, covered his brother with an extra blanket and, tears rolling down his cheeks, walked toward the door. He heard Qwan's voice, barely a whisper, and he turned to see his brother staring up at him with heavy-lidded eyes, trying to speak.

Then Jhoon walked out the door.

Alone in his shack, Jhoon was overwhelmed with guilt, the guilt he'd never been able to escape from. And together with the guilt came pain. His head was pounding. He buried his face into his mattress and covered the sides of his head with his hands, trying to shut out everything—everything that was inside and out.

chapter 18

Qwan shoved Jhoon's bandanna into his pocket. Outside he heard Billy's excited voice.

"Qwan, come here. Check this out."

Qwan walked out the door and turned to see Billy standing by the far side of the shelter.

"Look at this," Billy said, pointing to the area behind the shack.

A shallow grave with a small wooden marker had been dug between the cabin and the rock formation behind it. Qwan gazed down at the mound of dirt, his mind preoccupied.

"Who do you think it is?" Jarrod asked.

Qwan wasted no time replying. "The all-powerful Jack Mann."

Billy arched his eyebrows. "How do you know that?"

"Just a hunch." Qwan turned around to head back toward the boat when he heard a sound coming from behind the tall rock formation. He pressed up against the rock and peered through a hole. "Oh, my—"

Billy pushed in beside him and looked through the hole.

It was some kind of colony, with twenty, maybe thirty people, all dressed in rags, sitting and lying in the dirt and mud. Qwan heard some of them moaning as they tottered about amidst the stunted trees. Then one of the cloaked figures turned and spotted Qwan and Billy peering through the opening in the rocks. He raised his arms and groaned something that neither Qwan nor Billy could understand.

They took off through the clearing and ran all the way to the shore, where Jarrod was sitting beside the boat, waiting.

Qwan dragged the boat down to the lake, and Billy helped Jarrod inside. Under hazy moonlight, Qwan picked up the oars and began to row back.

chapter 19

Qwan, Billy, and Jarrod had left the boat where they had found it, climbed up the rugged cliff, and were now creeping down the pitch-black trail on their way back to Jarrod's tent, guided only by patches of moonlight. They were drawing near to the spot where they'd heard the noise and had seen the huge outline of what they thought might be Llao. Behind Qwan, Billy and Jarrod walked tentatively, Billy's eyes bouncing from one side of the forest to the other, Jarrod gripping the boy's lean shoulder.

The heat had finally lifted, and now occasional gusts of cool air blew at their backs.

Qwan was on a mission. He had been on one ever since he'd found the bandanna in the cabin on the island. He would confront his brother, Jhoon, in time, but first there was something else he had to do, something he wanted to do for everybody.

He headed right for the spot off the trail where

earlier he'd heard the noise. He wasn't sure what he would find, but he was confident enough to take the risk. Billy and Jarrod grew quiet as they approached the spot near "the rock," and when Billy saw Qwan enter the woods at the exact location where they'd spotted Llao, his bottom lip dropped nearly to the ground.

"What are you doing? Are you crazy?" He ran up behind Qwan, trying to pull him back onto the trail.

But Qwan shrugged Billy off and stepped into the dark mass of tall trees and dense shrubbery.

Billy ran back and took Jarrod's arm. "You ready?"

"Always," Jarrod replied, bringing his walking stick close to his body.

Hearts beating in double time, they followed their friend into the dark.

Qwan saw it almost immediately, and he felt a wave of heat rush through his body. It was the arm, rising up as high as the trees, darker than the night, a huge dark wing as large as the side of a house. Then he saw the other arm, an identical match, rising up on a diagonal, slicing through the trees. An eerie silence hung in the woods. Fighting off the fear that rose in the pit of his stomach, Qwan stood still, waiting for the creature to make its move. But the massive dark wings remained rigid.

Qwan moved closer, branches snapping under his feet, until he saw the entire body of the creature. And then he understood.

Billy and Jarrod stood about fifteen feet behind him. "What is it?" Jarrod whispered.

Qwan was now right in front of the thing. "It's a plane," he said, "a fighter plane." He walked up to where the cockpit had lodged itself into the ground. "It's upside down." He pointed to the giant black wings raised like arms. "The wings must have gotten caught in the trees, broke the fall—somewhat." He looked inside the cockpit.

"Uhh!" Qwan lurched away. A skeleton wearing a pilot's jumpsuit was hunched over in the cockpit. Qwan saw that the instruments on the panel had been smashed by bullets.

"What's wrong?" Billy asked.

Qwan continued backing away. "I just found the pilot's body."

"Whose plane was it?" Jarrod asked, his back against a tree.

"Can't tell," Qwan replied. "There's no markings. Besides, does it really matter?"

Jarrod grinned. "Well, I guess we've found Llao."

Qwan and Billy laughed, and the three made their way back onto the trail, Jarrod holding on to Qwan's shoulder.

They weren't on the path for ten seconds when they heard the sweeping sound. They froze in their steps. The noise had come from up ahead on the trail. Keeping perfectly still, the three watched as something emerged from the brush. For several moments none of the boys was able to even draw a breath.

A porcupine, its silver quills glistening under streaks of moonlight, waddled across the trail and vanished once again into the dark.

Qwan told Jarrod what it was, and the three shared another laugh before resuming their walk back to the tent.

They slept in Jarrod's tent that night, but Qwan had plans for the following morning and stayed up most of the night, thinking. He would leave early before the other two awoke, because this was a private matter, and he wanted to be alone to think about things before he arrived in the valley. The more he thought about Jhoon and the past four years, the angrier he became, until finally, in the late morning, he fell asleep.

chapter 20

It was early morning when Qwan came out of the woods overlooking the valley and gazed down at the shacks and tents of the Tribe. His mind had been racing ever since he'd left Jarrod's tent, and it was as if everything he'd passed along the way—the woods, Main Street, the creek—everything had been invisible to him, remote and indistinct. He hadn't noticed the threatening clouds rolling into Talima from the east or the cool air that came in gusts. He'd removed himself from such things because they would only take away from his focus, from the fury that consumed him, fury that had sustained him all these years.

He'd been thinking about his brother, Jhoon, picturing his face as he left the church that night so long ago, and thinking about the days he spent wandering the desert afterward, struggling to survive.

Taking a deep breath, he started down toward the dirt clearing on the valley floor, making a wide berth of the crude dwellings so as to not be seen on his way down. Some of the Tribe members were out, milling about a large dirt clearing on the valley floor. Some seemed to be drinking from cups, others were paired off, practicing self-defense techniques—the same techniques Qwan had first learned as a boy. As he drew nearer, Qwan recognized one of them as the man he'd fought in the street two nights ago, the African American with the bad knee.

A cool blast of air brushed against the back of his neck as he came to the bottom of the valley and walked toward the dirt clearing. He felt a drop of rain on his shoulder, and he looked up at the leaden sky. Another drop fell on his cheek, and then the drizzle became steady.

Those Tribe members standing around the perimeter of the ring were now looking straight at him. The African American had a dumbfounded expression on his face. Hands resting on his hips, he thrust out his head as if what he was looking at were a mirage.

Now only about a hundred feet away, Qwan noticed a girl with long dark hair sitting near the others. She rose abruptly and bounded into the ring, staring at Qwan as he approached, her hand shielding her eyes from the rain. She then turned, looked up at the dwellings behind her, and called out Jhoon's name.

Soon others piled out of their dwellings, jogged down the slope, and joined the rest. Everyone was out in the open, standing around the ring's perimeter, everyone but the occupant of the shack on top of the hill.

Fists clenched, Qwan now stepped into the ring.

The African American moved forward. "You've got a lot of nerve showing your face around here, thief."

"My fight is not with you," Qwan said, wiping rain from his eyes.

Peter met his gaze squarely. "I disagree."

He started circling Qwan, arms dangling by his sides. "Everybody out of the ring," Peter ordered. His eyes fixed on Qwan, he asked, "Do you know the rules of the ring, little man? It's simple: First one down loses."

Qwan stood motionless, watching as Peter advanced toward him. "I don't want to fight you," he said flatly.

"Suit yourself." Peter then lunged forward and threw a front snap kick, but Qwan moved to the side, slipping behind him.

Those standing around the ring began whispering to one another, occasionally glancing up at Jhoon's shack.

"I forgot how quick you are," Peter said, grinning. He moved in again, slowly, shifting one foot at a time, his guard up. When he was close enough, he threw a left jab, then came with a right cross, and then a round-house kick to the head.

Qwan slipped all three strikes, barely moving an inch. He smiled, seeing Peter was aggravated. *Soon,*

Qwan thought, *he will make a mistake, a mistake that will cost him the fight.*

And then it came.

Peter gave a loud grunt, turned sideways, and lunged at Qwan, kicking high with the outside edge of his foot leading the way.

Qwan saw it coming all along. He also saw that Peter's high kick had made him lose his balance. In one swift movement Qwan evaded the kick, dropped to the dirt, and swept Peter's other leg out from under him.

Peter fell back and landed hard in a newly formed puddle.

The Tribe grew so quiet only the pelting rain was heard. Then everyone began looking at one another, baffled, not knowing what to do next.

All at once Isabel and Ben came to life, rushing into the ring to help Peter off the ground. His face was contorted with pain as he hobbled away, one hand on his lower back.

"Who are you? What do you want?" Isabel's voice was harsh.

But Qwan didn't hear her because all of his attention was focused on the shack. His chest heaved under his drenched T-shirt, and he could take the waiting no longer. "Jhoon!" he cried.

Qwan was sure his brother had been watching, peering through the flap of his shack on the hill. But the longer he waited alone in the ring the more Qwan began to wonder if perhaps his brother had not been watching, or that he wasn't inside the shack, wasn't anywhere, that he'd disappeared the way he had years ago in the desert.

A peel of thunder cracked in the distance, then another, closer this time. The storm was moving swiftly over the desert toward Talima and the valley. Suddenly Ben bounded into the ring with raised fists, but Isabel jumped in front of him, pushing him back into the crowd. "No," she told him.

That's when Jhoon appeared.

Qwan recognized his brother's lean frame as he stood before the entrance of his shack, staring down into the ring.

A loud clap of thunder echoed through the valley, and the rain began to fall in heavy droplets. Some members of the tribe began chanting "Jhoon, Jhoon, Jhoon, Jhoon . . ."

Qwan watched his brother slowly descending the rugged slope. He wiped the rain from his face and tried to slow his breathing. When Jhoon reached the outside of the ring, the Tribe members parted, some looking straight into their leader's eyes, others down at the muddy, rain-lashed ground.

"Jhoon, Jhoon, Jhoon, Jhoon . . ."

Qwan felt the rage burning in his chest, coursing through his hands and feet. He wanted to scream at his brother louder than he'd ever screamed, empty his soul of all the hate he'd been storing up.

But the scream caught in his throat. He just stood there, directly opposite Jhoon, staring into his brother's eyes with a look of contempt.

Jhoon never looked back at him. His head was tilted forward, and his eyes scoured the brown puddles before him.

Qwan inched forward, unhurried, slightly to Jhoon's left, and Jhoon immediately started moving slowly to his right.

They were circling, waiting.

Crossing one leg over the other, Qwan began slowly to tighten the circle, his fists raised and clenched, his eyes never leaving his brother's. He was waiting for Jhoon to speak, to acknowledge his presence, to acknowledge everything. But his brother remained silent, and this angered Qwan even more, angered him so much that he had to let his brother know how he felt.

"Well, here comes the big hero," Qwan snarled. He looked over at the Tribe around the ring, then back at his brother. "Do they know that you left your own brother alone to die?" Qwan felt tears welling up in his eyes.

Around the perimeter of the ring members of the Tribe looked at one another with puzzled faces. Isabel covered her mouth with one hand.

Qwan felt his rage rising again. He wanted to expose his brother for the coward he was, but he didn't want to do it with words. He wanted to do it with his hands and feet. He also wanted to let Jhoon know that he knew the truth, and Qwan knew just how to do that.

"Jack Mann sent me here," Qwan said, smiling at his brother.

Now he had his attention.

Jhoon's heart raced. "You're lying," he said defiantly.

"Maybe," Qwan replied, "maybe not." And with that Qwan pulled Jhoon's old bandanna from his pocket and calmly tied it around his forehead. Then he stared at his brother. "The only thing you learned from Dad was how to tell stories." Qwan paused for a moment, then grinned. "I'm the one who learned how to fight."

Jhoon met Qwan's gaze squarely, sucking in his upper lip. He sprang forward, feigning with his hands. "Prove it!" he dared.

Qwan met him in the center of the ring, faked a back fist punch to Jhoon's face, then dropped to the ground, spun around, and tried to take out Jhoon's planted leg with a sweep.

But Jhoon lifted his leg clear of Qwan's sweep and came back at him with a front snap kick targeted for Qwan's chest. Qwan blocked the kick with his forearm, which is precisely what Jhoon had wanted him to do. When he saw Qwan's face unguarded, he whipped his leg out in an arc and caught his brother squarely on the jaw.

The blow stung Qwan's cheek and rattled his teeth. Then before he could regain his composure, Jhoon struck again, spinning so that his back was toward Qwan and letting go with a back kick that stuck firmly in Qwan's gut like a spear.

Qwan felt the air rush out of him. He stumbled back, losing his balance, almost slipping in a puddle.

He did stay on his feet, but he was growing nervous, unsure of himself. Jhoon's speed and confidence were daunting, and his kicks were harder, bringing more pain than any Qwan had ever felt. What if, unlike all the others he'd fought, Jhoon would not make a mistake?

Jhoon stepped forward with an axe kick, raising his leg straight up in the air and coming down in a chopping-like motion that would have snapped Qwan's collar bone.

But Qwan turned at the last moment and evaded the devastating blow. Regaining a measure of confidence, he sharpened his gaze on Jhoon, who had dropped his hands to his side in a show of cockiness.

So Qwan struck while he had the chance. He leaped in the air and delivered an awesome flying side kick that caught Jhoon by surprise and struck him in the nose. Jhoon managed to stay on his feet, but blood trickled from one nostril. He shook his head and pushed back his wet hair. Then he skipped forward and flung out a round-house kick aimed at Qwan's ribs. But the kick missed because Qwan had stepped away, stepped in the same direction of the kick, and countered with a punishing hook kick that landed on Jhoon's cheek.

"Way to go, Qwan!" a voice rang out.

Qwan turned and saw Billy and Jarrod standing behind him, alone on the opposite side of the ring.

A loud murmur rose from the crowd. This was the first time the Tribe had seen their leader hit so hard.

"Come on, brother," Qwan said in a mocking tone. "Show everybody what a warrior you are now." Rain sprayed in his face, and his voice was garbled as all his anger erupted and tears began to fall from his eyes. "Why did you leave me, Jhoon?" Qwan insisted, his voice breaking. "How could you leave your own brother like that?"

"You were sick," Jhoon yelled. "I thought you were going to die. I couldn't watch—"

"You're a coward!" Qwan snarled.

A bolt of lightning lit up the valley. For a moment neither brother seemed to know what to do or say.

Then Jhoon charged, out of control, his arms pumping, leaving himself wide open as he reached Qwan.

The spinning hook kick. A dangerous and risky weapon if not used correctly, a devastating strike if mastered. It was Qwan's specialty, a deadly secret hidden in the muscles of his right leg. Over the years he'd practiced the kick hundreds of thousands of times, refining it to perfection. He could throw it in his sleep—the pivoting of the front foot—heel out—toward the opponent, the backward spin, then the back leg whipping out and up, swinging with great velocity at the opponent. The kick had become like a close friend, a reliable and deadly friend.

And when Jhoon was two feet in front of him, charging fast, hands reaching out, Qwan pivoted on his front foot, spun around and in the same motion released his deadly friend.

There was a moment before the kick landed, a stolen moment when Qwan's face was only inches from Jhoon's. And in that moment Qwan looked unflinchingly at his brother and saw himself mirrored in Jhoon's eyes, saw the fear and regret and the heartache—saw the void caused by separation.

Then Qwan's foot struck Jhoon on the side of the head. The kick drove Jhoon several feet through the air before he fell to the mud in a heap.

A hush settled over the Tribe. Isabel ran into the ring and lifted Jhoon's head out of a puddle. But Qwan got in between her and Jhoon, reaching behind his brother's head and under his arm and lifting him into a sitting position.

Jhoon was conscious—dazed—but conscious. A bright red oval marked the flesh where the kick had landed. He looked up at Qwan, threw his arm around his younger brother's shoulders, then closed his eyes.

Qwan

Rain lashed the ground as Qwan helped his brother to his feet and began walking slowly through the puddles of mud and out of the ring. As Qwan passed by Billy and Jarrod, he put a hand on Billy's shoulder and told him to stay with Jarrod, that he would see him tomorrow and explain everything then.

Then Qwan led his brother past the others and up to the shack on the hill.

In the dry dwelling, he helped Jhoon onto the mattress, then took a seat on the ground at his brother's feet. Rain pelted the roof and rattled the side wall. For a long while neither brother said a word. Jhoon had rolled over onto one side, looking away from Qwan. Then, after what seemed like days, he spoke.

"I'm sorry, Qwan," he said in a mournful tone. "I'm more sorry than you could ever know."

Qwan felt as though he might break down and cry, long and hard cries. But it wasn't time for that.

As the hours passed and the rain continued to lash against the walls and roof of the shack, Qwan felt the anger, which had been a part of him for so many years, slowly lifting, and a sense of tranquillity began to envelop him. There was a lot to talk about, a lot of things that needed to be cleared up. But they would have to wait. For now he was at ease.

After several hours of silence, Qwan stood up, walked to the mattress, and lay down next to his brother.

That night they slept side by side. And for the first time since they were last together, they dreamed of life before the war.

Acknowledgments

Many thanks to the people who made this book possible: Rena Copperman, David Griffith, Jonathan Freund, Barbara Schoichet, Lindsey Hay, Walia Artenstein, Sasha Santander, Mashenka Lebedynec, Neal Yamamoto, Stephen Guadagno, and last but certainly not least, the redoubtable J. M. Hoffe.